COURAGE

A HEROES OF BIG SKY NOVEL

KRISTEN PROBY

AMPERSAND PUBLISHING, INC.

Courage

A Heroes of Big Sky Novel

By

Kristen Proby

COURAGE

A Big Sky Novel - Heroes of Big Sky

Kristen Proby

Copyright © 2021 by Kristen Proby

Cover Design: By Hang Le

Cover Image by Wander Aguiar Photography

Published by Ampersand Publishing, Inc.

Paperback ISBN: 978-1-63350-101-0

Dedicated to Monica Murphy and Devney Perry, my
sprinting partners, my confidants,
my friends.
Thank you. For everything.

PROLOGUE

~NATASHA~

"*A*untie Tash," Kevin says, holding out his hand covered in honey Greek yogurt. "Wash me."

"Holy cow, how did you do that?" I hurry over with a wet washcloth and wipe down Kev's fingers, then glance over at his twin sister, Kelsey. "That doesn't go in your hair, sugar."

She laughs and rubs yogurt on the side of her head. "I'm washing it."

"Your hair?"

She nods, and I blow a lock of hair out of my face. Where is my scrunchie?

"Yeah. I'm washing it."

I groan and check my phone for the fifteenth time this morning. Where are they? Monica, my very best friend in the world, and her husband, Rich, left the kids with me overnight so they could have a romantic evening alone. They even went to a rental house up on

Whitetail Mountain. A fancy place with a pool, where they could enjoy each other and have all the sex in the world.

And I kept the twins—which I don't mind at all. I love these two. But, man, they're a handful. And Monica was supposed to be here two hours ago.

"Auntie Tash," Kelsey says. "I want more oranges."

"Okay. I can do that." I recheck my phone before retrieving some orange slices from the cutting board in my destroyed kitchen.

We watched movies last night for our slumber party. When you're entertaining four-year-olds, it's important to have a wide array of snacks on hand for movie watching.

And the remnants of those snacks are still spread all over my kitchen.

As much as I love them both, I can't wait for Monica to pick them up so I can clean this hellhole and then take a long nap.

How she does it with twins, I'll never know.

I check my phone again, and there's nothing.

"They *were* coming back this morning, right?" I double-check my calendar. Sure enough, it's right there. *Monica back.* She harassed me forever the first night, checking on the kids. I finally had to tell her to stop bugging me and go attack her husband.

She called once yesterday to say hi to the twins.

And I haven't heard from her since.

When noon rolls around, and Monica is now

several hours late, I decide to call Sam, Monica's brother.

It rings five times before he picks up.

"Yeah," he says.

"Hey. Are you swamped?"

"Yeah, I'm getting all my stuff packed up today. Moving next week."

"Oh, right." Sam took a new firefighter position in Spokane. It's only four hours away, but the thought of him not living in Cunningham Falls anymore is a punch to the gut. "So, your house sold, then?"

"Yep. I close on Monday. I'm getting everything into storage for now. Are you okay?"

"I'm fine, but something's weird. I'm watching the twins this weekend so Monica and Rich could have some *alone* time. They were supposed to be here to get the kids this morning, and I haven't heard from them. She's not answering. And, honestly, I'm getting worried."

"Do you know where they were staying?"

"Yeah, she gave me the address just in case."

"Text it to me. I'll take a break here and go check on them. But if I see my sister naked because she and Rich are getting in one more round of sex, I'll kill you dead."

"Deal. Thanks, Sam. I'm sorry to interrupt your day."

"I could use a break anyway. I'll keep you posted."

"Great. Thanks."

He hangs up, and I turn to the kids with a forced smile.

"Where's my mommy?" Kelsey asks. "I want to go home."

"I know. They'll be here shortly. They probably just lost track of time, that's all. Why don't I put a movie on for you guys while we wait?"

"*Scooby-Doo*," Kevin says as he jumps out of his chair and runs for the living room. "Let's watch *Scooby-Doo*!"

I follow the kids and get them settled with Scooby, then pace back to the kitchen. I take a deep breath and let it out slowly.

I have a bad feeling. My stomach roils. I feel hot.

Something is *wrong*.

"Please, let me be wrong." I stare at my phone, willing it to ring. Finally, it lights up with Sam's name.

I answer immediately. "Hey."

"Tash." He clears his throat, and I instinctively know that I was right.

"No."

"Jesus, I don't know what to say."

"No, Sam. No."

"Honey, you need to call someone to come be with you. I'm going to be a while up here with them."

"What happened?" I cradle the phone against my ear.

"I'm not sure."

"No." I shake my head and sit on the floor behind

the island where the kids can't see me. "Please. You're wrong."

"I'll be there in a couple of hours. Call Aspen. Is Aspen in town?"

I nod, even though he can't see me. Aspen, one of our closest friends, has been in town all winter. "Yeah. I think so."

"Call her. I don't want you to be alone right now. I'll be there when I can."

"What do I tell the babies?"

He's quiet for a moment. "Nothing yet. We'll talk to them together. Call Aspen."

He hangs up, and all I can do is sit and cry. How? How can this be happening? They just wanted a weekend away.

I dial Aspen's number.

"Hi, friend."

"I need you. Right now."

"I'm on my way."

CHAPTER 1

~NATASHA~

One month later...

"Carbon monoxide poisoning."

I keep my back turned to the two busy-bodies gossiping in the produce section. As if the past month hasn't been hard enough, I get this just about everywhere I go. Murmurs, whispers behind my back. Looks of pity. Words of sympathy.

Leaving the house has been pure torture to begin with, but adding this onto the stress of it makes me want to hide under the covers and never come out.

"So sad," the other one, Misty, says. "They just fell asleep and never woke up."

Just when I'm about to turn to the women and say,

"Really? I'm right here," my phone rings, grabbing my attention.

"Hello?"

"Hi, Tash, this is Hilda Smith at the school. I'm afraid I need to see you and Mr. Waters in my office as soon as you can get here."

"Is something wrong? Is one of the twins hurt?"

"No, no, it's nothing like that. We have a behavioral issue to discuss. I'd really prefer to talk to you and Sam together."

I blow out a breath and stare at the basket full of groceries. "I can be there in about thirty minutes."

"I'll see you then."

She hangs up, and I resign myself to not finishing today's grocery run. Instead, I make my way to the checkout.

Once the groceries are paid for, I hurry home to put the perishables in the fridge, leaving the rest for later.

This isn't the first time in the past month we've been called in for a meeting with the school. Both kids have had a tough time adjusting.

Hell, *I'm* having a tough time, and I'm over thirty.

Just as I pull into the parking lot, I see Sam parking his blue truck. He waits for me on the sidewalk.

"I always feel like *I'm* the one in trouble," he says grimly as we walk toward the front door of the building.

It's summer, so the kids aren't in school yet. They start kindergarten in a few weeks, but Monica enrolled them in preschool all summer, and we thought it would be best if we tried to keep their schedules as close to normal as possible.

And, I can admit, I need the few hours during the day to get caught up on everything that I can't see to when the two of them are underfoot.

And, yes, that makes me feel inadequate and horrible.

"If Kevin's stealing again, I'll kill him," I mutter.

Sam doesn't reply, just takes my hand in that patient, sturdy way he has that tells me everything will be okay.

"I'll take them tonight," he says.

"It's not your night," I remind him. "We'll be okay."

"Let's find out what's going on before you turn me down on the offer," he suggests as we reach the office doorway. "Hi, Hilda."

The older woman, who happened to teach *me* in middle school, glances up and smiles. "Hello, you two. Come on in."

I have a feeling the warm welcome is only to butter us up for what's about to happen.

"Don't keep us in suspense," I say immediately, sitting on the edge of the seat as if I'm ready to take off running at any second. "What happened?"

"It's been a series of events today, I'm afraid," she says. "Kelsey won't talk."

"I'm sorry, what?" Sam asks.

"She won't speak. Won't answer questions or even

talk to her friends. She just shakes her head and looks at the floor or ground. Her teacher says this was not the case yesterday."

"It wasn't the case this morning, either," I say and rub my fingers across my forehead. "What else?"

"Kevin peed on the playground during recess."

Sam and I just stare at the woman. Finally, Sam laughs.

I hang my head in my hands.

"Listen, you two," Hilda continues, "I know that it's only been a month since the twins lost their parents, and that you both are doing the very best you can. I can't even begin to imagine the grief and pain you're all going through. But I have to be honest here. We just can't have this behavior continue. It's disruptive to the rest of the students. And, frankly, it's difficult for the teachers to handle."

"I get it." I sigh and glance at Sam, who's no longer laughing. "Can you please give us another chance? Just one more. It's Friday. Let us take the weekend to talk to the kids and see if we can get some of this resolved so they're not acting out at school. I know they enjoy it here. They talk about it all evening."

Hilda sits back and watches us. I can see it written all over her face that she'd already made up her mind to kick them out.

But she sighs and nods. "Okay. One more chance. But if anything like this happens again, I'll have no choice."

"Understood," Sam says. "Thank you for your patience, Hilda. We appreciate it. Are they ready for us to take them home?"

"Yes, they should be waiting just outside. Class was dismissed. Good luck."

We stand to leave. When I see the kids silently sitting in their chairs, their blue eyes big and haunted, I want to break down and cry.

Instead, I offer them my hands.

"Come on. Let's go home."

We're quiet as all four of us walk to my car. Once the twins are settled in their seats, I close the door and turn to Sam.

"I'm sure you had better plans, but are you interested in coming home with us?"

"I'll be right behind you."

"Thanks."

Before *it* happened, the kids used to chat incessantly whenever I picked them up from school, which was a couple of times a week because of Monica's and Rich's busy work schedules. But over the past month, we've sat in so much silence, it almost feels like it screams.

I've barely put my car in park when Kevin unbuckles himself from his seat and hurries out of the car, running toward the house.

Kelsey doesn't move at all.

"We're home, sugar."

She turns those haunted eyes to me. "Okay."

"Let's go have a snack and talk with Uncle Sam,

okay?"

She nods and waits for me to help her out of her seat, even though she's perfectly capable of doing it herself. But I don't mind. Once she's free of the belt, she wraps her little arms around my neck and gives me a big hug.

"Don't die, okay?"

I turn my face to look at her in surprise.

"What?"

"Don't die."

"Oh, honey." I kiss her little cheek and carry her out of the car. "I'm right here. Let's go get that snack."

She rests her head on my shoulder, and I walk toward the front porch where Sam and Kevin are waiting for us.

"We heard you two had a busy day today," I begin after I unlock the door and everyone files into my small house. "Who wants to talk about it?"

No one says a word.

"Okay, so none of us *wants* to, but we have to."

"Why?" Kevin asks.

"Because we need to have a family meeting to figure some stuff out," Sam replies. "You two know right and wrong. You know when you're being bad. And when you're hurting someone's feelings. Right?"

Both of them nod mournfully.

"Then why are you acting this way?" I ask. "I know you're sad. I am, too. But we can't be mean to other people."

"It doesn't matter." Kevin glares at the floor. He just turned five and has so much anger in his little body, I don't know what to do.

"It matters," Sam corrects him. "No iPad tonight."

Kevin just hops off his chair and walks to his bedroom.

"Can I have a nap?" Kelsey asks. "I'm sleepy."

"Sure." I brush her hair off her shoulder. "Do you want me to read to you first?"

"No. I'll just sleep."

She walks away to the room she shares with her brother, leaving me with Sam.

"I'm fucking this up," I say and rub my hands over my face. "Big time."

"They need counseling," he says. "Shit, we all do."

"What was she thinking, leaving them to me?" I ask. I look at Sam and hold my hands out at my sides. "I don't know how to be a mom."

"Well, I don't know how to be a dad, but they left them to me, too. They trusted us to do what's right. And we're doing that."

I want to tell him that shuffling them back and forth between my house and his rental isn't exactly the best thing for them, but I don't. Because we're doing the best we can with the hand we've been dealt.

And it's a pretty shitty one.

"I'm going to stay for a while," he says. "I'll have dinner with you guys. I don't have other plans."

"We'd like that. Thank you."

"You don't have to thank me. But you could make your famous tacos."

I smile, but it doesn't reach my eyes. Monica loved my tacos.

"Deal."

"Let's grab lunch," Sam suggests a week later. We just finished signing the papers to sell the salon, one of the last details to see to regarding the estate.

I shrug a shoulder. "I'm really not that hungry."

"You have to eat," he says gently. "And so do I. The kids are with Aspen. Let's go be crazy and eat junk food at Ed's."

Ed's Diner is my favorite. He knows this.

And it totally works.

"Yeah, okay. Let's do it. Shall we walk over?"

"Good idea."

The diner isn't too far away from the title office we just left, so we set off on foot, soaking in the sunshine.

"I feel guilty for selling the salon," I say and watch as a kid on a bicycle zooms past us.

"You said you didn't want to continue running it," he points out.

Poor Sam. I've been so up and down over the past month, I'm surprised he hasn't shaken me silly. Instead, he's been kind and patient.

And hot, but I'm so exhausted, even my libido has gone on vacation.

"I don't want to run it," I agree. "And I'm certainly not in the right headspace to hire someone else to do it. I know that selling was the right call, and Reagan will do a wonderful job. Also, Monica used her inheritance when your parents passed away to start the business. This way, that money will go into a trust for the kids. It's the right thing to do."

"Then why do you feel guilty?"

"I live my life in a permanent state of guilt." Sam reaches over to take my hand and gives it a squeeze. "And I know that Monica would roll her eyes and tell me to get over it. To *stop* it. But I can't."

"It hasn't been long," he reminds me gently and pulls me to a stop so I don't walk out in front of traffic. "Red light."

"Oops, thanks. I'm going to just enjoy a greasy cheeseburger and your company."

"Good plan. I'll do the same."

We hurry across the street and into Ed's, which is surprisingly quiet for near lunchtime. There's almost always a wait to be seated because it's so popular— among the locals and tourists alike.

But today, luck is on our side and the hostess immediately shows us to a booth against the windows.

Ed's has been in business for longer than either of us has been alive. Ed himself still runs the kitchen, and little about the place has changed in decades. It's an old-fashioned diner, just like in the movies, with red vinyl seats, a long soda fountain bar, and a jukebox in the corner that plays everything from Elvis to Bon Jovi.

Ed claims he won't put any music in that thing that was made after 1990.

This diner has been an integral part of my life. We came here for birthday dinners when I was a kid, and after football games in high school. I sat at a nearby table and mooned over Sam as he joked around with his friends across the room.

And this was where Monica told me and Aspen that she was pregnant with the twins.

I take a deep breath and set the menu aside. I don't have to look at it to know what I want.

"Hey, you two," Flo, another staple at Ed's, says as she approaches our table to take our order. "What can I getcha?"

"I'll have a cheeseburger, no tomato, with fries and mayo on the side. A Coke to drink, please." I smile at Flo as she writes down my order and then turns to Sam.

"I think I'm in the mood for the BLT, onion rings, and a Coke, as well. Thanks, Flo."

"You got it. Shouldn't take long." She winks and walks away.

"Okay, I admit it. Now that we're here, I'm hungry."

Sam grins. "You can never resist Ed's."

"It's true. It's a drug, and I'm completely addicted. How are things at work? I haven't even asked you what's happening with the position in Spokane. I'm sorry. I'm a shitty friend."

"Nah, we've had a bit on our minds." He shakes his head and rubs his lips together. "The guys in Spokane said they'd hold the position for me for six months. And, of course, the job here didn't want to lose me in the first place, so everything's fine."

"But you sold your house and everything."

"I'm renting the apartment." He shrugs. "Honestly, I'm okay. Pissed most of the time, but fine."

"You hide the anger well."

"The punching bag at the gym would argue with that."

I glance around the room and notice that a couple of people are looking our way.

"You know what the worst part of living in a small town is?" I ask him after our drinks are delivered.

"The gossip." He sips his Coke and also glances around. "We should be used to it by now."

"It's never really been aimed at me before," I admit and squirm in my seat.

"I think people mean well," he says. "They feel bad."

"And they think I don't have ears. Every time I go to the grocery, bank, or...*anywhere*, they talk as if I'm not even there. *'Oh, isn't it sad? Poor Sam and Tash. Stuck with those babies.'* I'm not *stuck* with anything."

"People say that?"

"Oh, yeah. And other things. Why can't they just talk behind my back when I'm not around like normal people? I don't honestly care about that, I just don't want to hear it."

"I'm tired of the constant condolences," Sam says. "If I hear *'I'm sorry for your loss'* one more time, I might strangle someone."

"Amen to that."

Our food is delivered, and my mouth starts to water.

"Nothing like a burger from Ed's." I go through the ritual of taking the lettuce off and rearranging the pickles, squirting ketchup into my mayo before giving it a stir with a fry. When I look up, I see Sam watching me with a grin. "What?"

"If you don't want the lettuce, why don't you ask them to hold it with the tomato?"

"Because this is how I do it." I munch on a fry. "It's my routine. My Ed's routine."

"Okay." He takes an onion ring and reaches over to dunk it in my sauce, but I slap his hand. "Hey. Don't be stingy."

"Get your own." But I laugh and scoot the little dish closer to him. "Okay, I'll share."

"That looks beautiful on you."

I blink at him. "What?"

"The laugh. I think it's the first time I've seen it since…the day."

I shrug a shoulder. "I haven't felt much like laughing."

And when I do, the guilt settles in again.

Monica doesn't get to laugh anymore, why should I?

Because I'm alive.

"Okay, I won't mention it again because you stopped laughing and now you look sad again."

"I'm okay." I take a big bite of burger. "This helps."

I have to wipe ketchup off my chin.

"You're so classy," he says with a laugh.

"I know, right?"

"Hey, you guys." We look up to find Mrs. Blakely standing at our table. She owns Little Deli on main street and was close to Sam's parents when they were alive. "I don't want to interrupt your lunch, I just wanted to stop by and see how you're holding up."

Here we go.

"We're doing fine, thank you for asking," Sam says in his polite voice. The one his parents taught him to use whenever speaking to an *elder*.

"Well, I'm sure you're doing as well as you can, considering," Mrs. Blakely says and gives his shoulder a soft pat. Then she turns her gaze to me, and I feel like squirming again. "How about you, dear? I'm sure the twins are giving you a run for your money."

"They're great." I swallow the bite of burger that now tastes like cardboard.

"I've heard they're having some trouble at the preschool," she says, and I sigh.

For fuck's sake, all I wanted to do was have lunch with Sam.

"You know what, I don't think I'm hungry anymore." I wipe my mouth and drop the napkin on the table. Sam sits back in his seat, anger warring with worry as he watches me. "Mrs. Blakely, you already paid your respects at the funeral. There's no need to interrupt us during lunch and make us sad. Make us feel *badly* all over again. It's rude. And it's not okay."

I push out of the booth and head for the door.

"Oh, my," I hear her say, but I don't give a shit.

This is why I rarely leave the house.

Because every damn time I do, I'm reminded that my best friend is gone, and she's never coming back. She won't get to see her gorgeous children grow up. She was robbed of everything.

All because a fucking landlord didn't install a CO2 detector in a rental house.

"Tash."

I hear Sam rush up behind me. He doesn't take my arm, he simply wraps his arms around me and hugs me close from behind.

"I'm just so *angry*," I whisper.

"I know. Me, too. They're wrapping up our food to go. Let's go home and eat in peace there."

I nod as he turns me around to face him.

"I was rude to her."

"She'll survive." He kisses my forehead, and tiny sparks of awareness appear in my belly, making me swallow hard. "Let's go."

CHAPTER 2

~SAM~

*B*am!

I slam my fist into the punching bag and imagine that it's the fucking landlord's face. The asshole who killed my sister.

I hit, jab, and punch until the muscles in my arms and across my shoulders sing from the impacts. When I take a break and turn to sip some water, I see Noah King sitting on the bench behind me, tying his shoes and watching me silently.

Noah's a friend. But I wasn't expecting company.

Then again, I don't own this gym.

"Hey, man." I wipe the sweat off my brow with a towel. "You need the bag?"

"Nah, I'm lifting today," he says as he stands, but he doesn't walk toward the weights. "How's it going, man?"

I shrug a shoulder and adjust my sparring gloves. "Same ol'."

He raises a brow. "Bullshit."

"I'm worried about Tash," I admit with a sigh. "She's all over the place with her moods, and I know she's overwhelmed with having the kids full time. I take them when I'm not on call, but you know how it is around here. I'm almost always on call. She puts on a brave face for the twins, but when they're not around, she just crumbles. She's full of guilt and hasn't even had time to grieve. Not really, you know?"

He nods thoughtfully. "Yeah, that's rough. Kids are hard. Fallon's pregnant with our second, and I'm scared to death."

"You make beautiful babies," I remind him. "And you have plenty of space out on your property to have a dozen."

He laughs and shakes his head. "Don't let Fallon hear you say that. She swears we're done at two. So, you told me how Tash is doing. Now, how are *you*?"

I stop and blink at him. "I just—"

"Bullshit." His face is expressionless as he stares back at me. I sigh.

"I'm fucked up in the head. Overwhelmed. Guilty. Pissed as all hell." I punch the bag once more. "I want someone to *pay*, and I know they never will. Because it's considered a goddamn accident."

"I'm quite sure old man Betters didn't mean—"

"It was fucking irresponsible," I interrupt. "And it cost me two people I love."

"I know." The words are quiet as Noah nods. "You're right."

I swallow and shove the bitterness down. "I can't, Noah. I can't deal with all of this bullshit right now. I have too much on my plate. I have kids now, and a demanding career, and another job that I don't even know for sure if I can take. I don't have the luxury of swimming in my feelings right now."

"So you hit the bag instead."

"Yeah." I shrug again. "It's cheap therapy. Seems to do the trick."

"Then I say punch away." He stands and pats me on the shoulder. "I'm always around, you know. For anything. Even to take the kids for a little while. Fallon and I would love to have them. We can take them to the sanctuary and show them the birds."

Noah owns and runs the Spread Your Wings wild bird sanctuary just outside of town. It's a cool place. The kids would love it.

"I may take you up on that sometime."

"Do. We'll take the kids, and you can do something nice for Natasha. I know you're not a couple, but I'm sure she could use some time out of the house without the twins in tow."

My gut clenches at the *you're not a couple*. Why? Of course, we're not a couple.

But I smile and nod at my friend. "Thank you. Really. I'll keep it in mind."

Noah moves away to get his workout started, and I take off my gloves, done for the day.

I punched the bag so hard; it's a wonder it's still hanging.

Maybe I should take Noah up on his offer to watch the kids and do something nice for Tash. God knows she could use it, and so could I.

An idea starts to form as I grab my duffel, bypass the locker room and head straight for my truck. I'll shower at the station.

But before I can even start the vehicle, I get a call.

From Tash.

"Hey," I say into the phone but have to pull it away from my head because of the deafening screams blaring in my ears. "Hey, what's going on?"

"Can you swing by real quick?"

"On my way."

I hang up and start the truck, my mind already running through all of the horrible things that could be happening at Tash's house.

Is someone cut? Bleeding out?

Did they fall and break a leg, their bone sticking out through the tender flesh?

I've seen too much on my job. It could literally be anything.

I come to a screeching halt in front of Tash's house

and sprint up to the front door, bursting inside to find both twins crying in the living room.

"What's wrong? What's going on? Where's Auntie Tash?"

"In here," she calls from the bathroom. I run down the hall and skid to a stop, taking in the scene. "I hope you don't have a queasy stomach."

"You're bleeding." I see a laceration across the palm of her hand. My EMT brain immediately takes over, and I grab a towel to clean away the blood so I can see what I'm dealing with here. "How?"

"I was cutting fruit for breakfast, and Kevin bumped into my arm. And, well... You see what happened. They're upset, and I can't stop this bleeding."

"Because you need stitches." I wrap her palm with the towel. "Keep pressure on it. I'm taking you to the ER."

"I have to get the kids to preschool."

"They're in no shape to go to school this morning, Tash. They're upset and worried about you. I'm calling Aspen to come sit with them."

"She's done too much," Tash says with a sigh. "I can't keep asking her to come running over to help. It's been *two months*, Sam. There comes a time when I have to be able to take care of my life. Without calling in the troops every time someone cries, or I cut my hand."

"That's what they're there for," I remind her gently and brush my fingers down her cheek. Her skin is so damn soft. "Aspen would be pissed if she heard you say that, by the way."

"Yeah, well. Okay. We'll call her. But she's probably at Drips today. She has a business to run."

"She has a manager for that," I remind her. "And she's married to a damn prince. I think she can afford to take a morning off."

I'm already calling Aspen's number.

"Hey, Sam. How's it going?"

"Oh, you know. Never a dull moment around here." I quickly run down what's happening. "Do you have time to take the kids for a couple of hours while we have her hand seen to?"

"Of course. Actually, I'm on my way to Drips. I'll swing by and pick them up. They can come with me. I'll put them to work."

"Sounds damn good to me."

"See you in five."

"I heard," Tash says when I hang up. "Thanks."

She holds her towel-wrapped hand against her chest as we walk down the hall and find the kids still sitting in the living room, sniffling.

"Hey, no need to cry," Tash says and kisses their heads. "I'm going to be just fine. It's just a cut on my hand."

"I didn't mean to," Kevin says and clings to her. "I'm so sorry."

"Of course, you didn't mean to," Tash assures him.

"Uncle Sam is here, and he's an expert in these things. He thinks I should go have a doctor have a look at it."

"How about instead of going to school today, you go spend some time with Aspen?" I ask the kids and see their eyes light up. "She's going to take you to the coffee shop."

"Okay," Kelsey says. She's always been the more laid-back of the two.

"I want to go with Auntie," Kevin says, still clinging to her hip.

"We won't be long," Tash assures and squats down next to him. "And when we get home, you and I can curl up and watch a movie, okay?"

He nods, and I hear Aspen pull into the drive. "Okay, let's go."

"Hi, guys," Aspen says with a smile when we all come outside. "What a fun surprise."

"Thanks," Tash says with an apologetic grin. "Sam says I need stitches."

"Ouch," Aspen replies. "Well, don't rush on my account. I've got things handled with these little monsters."

They pile into Aspen's SUV, and I lead Tash to my truck.

"This throbs like a bitch," she says when I boost her up onto the seat and buckle her in.

I accidentally brush her breast with my arm and feel the contact all the way to my cock.

Jesus, when did Tash turn into a sexy, curvy woman?

I've always seen her as my little sister's friend. That's it.

But now that we've been in close quarters for the past couple of months, I'm seeing her differently.

Maybe it's just my long-ignored libido talking.

But I don't think so.

"Sam?" Her breath is on my neck. I didn't realize that I'd frozen in place. "You okay?"

"Sorry," I mutter and click the belt into place. "Spacey today, I guess."

I shut the door and hurry around to the driver's side.

"Let's get you all fixed up."

"THE END." I close the book and kiss Kelsey on the forehead. "That's it for tonight. You both need to get some sleep."

"Just *one* more story?" Kevin asks from the twin bed across the room.

"I read four stories, and that's one more than usual. Because you were extra-good for Aspen today. Thanks for that, by the way."

"It was fun," Kelsey says, her big blue eyes droopy with sleep. "She let us have a cookie."

"That was nice of her." I can't help but lean over and kiss her little cheek.

"Is Auntie Tash's hand really okay?" Kevin asks. Even though this dude has given us a lot of trouble over the past couple of months, he's been so worried today. He loves Tash. They both do.

"Yes. The doctor stitched her right up. She's going to be sore for a couple of days, but it'll heal."

There's no need to tell them how she fainted when they brought out the needle for the stitches.

That'll be our little secret.

"Okay." Kevin snuggles down under the covers. "Good night."

I cross to him and kiss his head. "Good night, buddy."

After I turn out the light, I close the door and walk down the hall. I find Tash in the kitchen, emptying the dishwasher with one hand.

"Let me." I scoot her aside and start pulling out glasses and mugs. "You should rest."

"It's just my hand," she reminds me but doesn't argue about stepping aside as she leans against the kitchen island. "Did they fight you at all?"

"Not much. I read an extra story. Where does this go?" I hold up a colander.

She points to a cabinet, and I stow it away. "How does it feel?"

"Aches like a bitch," she says. "Now that the numbing stuff has worn off."

29

"He gave you pain meds. Take one."

"No." She shakes her head. "I'll take ibuprofen or something. I have the kids. I can't take the hard stuff. What if they needed me and I'm out cold? Not gonna happen."

I empty the silverware tray. "Jeez, you go through the spoons."

"No kidding. I'm gonna buy more."

I turn and look at her. She's in black leggings that mold to the curves of her thighs and ass and a baggy sweatshirt.

Tash is tall, not much shorter than my six feet. With that slender, willowy body and curves in all the right places, she's sexy as hell.

And as I watch, the neck of her sweatshirt falls over her shoulder.

No bra strap.

Jesus.

I could just push my hand under the hemline and feel her bare skin.

She raises her face, and her dark eyes find mine.

"You okay?" she asks, tilting her head.

"Yeah." I clear my throat and get back to the task at hand. Once the dishes are all put away, I load the dishwasher with the dirty ones in the sink, start it, and then wipe down the counters.

"Thanks." She yawns widely. "Wanna sit and chat for a while, or are you ready to head home? I'm sure you're tired."

"I can stay for a few."

I toss the towel onto the counter and follow her into the living room. She sits in the corner of the couch, and I take the opposite side.

"Thanks for staying all day," she says. "You didn't have to."

"No biggie. I called the chief and asked him to take me off the board for the day."

Her eyes go wide. "Wait. You took the day off? Shit, Sam, I'm sorry. I need to write down your schedule so I don't bother you on your working days."

"Hey, it's fine. I'm happy to help, you know that."

She shakes her head and then sighs. "You know, some days I think I have this all under control. On the days when the kids are happy, and I'm caught up on laundry and get no calls from the school. They're few but coming more often than they did in the beginning —which I think is a good sign."

"Definitely a good sign."

"And then days like today just sneak up on me and slap me across the face as if God is saying, *'Ha! You thought you could do this? Think again, sweetheart.'*"

"What are you talking about? You did great today. You got hurt, you called me, we executed a plan. It all came together."

"But you had to take off of work."

"And if that had been an issue, I would have said something. Tash, I'm not here because I feel sorry for you or something. The kids are my responsibility, too, you know."

"But I'm not."

"Aren't you?"

The words are out of my mouth before I can stop them. She narrows her gorgeous dark eyes, and that sass she's always been known for comes to the surface.

I much prefer the sass to the sadness.

"I don't need you to save me, Sam Waters."

"No, ma'am." I chuckle and shake my head. "Absolutely, not. But I can be here because I *want* to be, can't I? If not, just tell me to get lost. It'll wound my ego, but I'll survive."

"You can be here anytime you want," she says with a laugh. "I just don't want you to feel *obligated.* I know we're co-parenting the twins. And that's awesome because I couldn't do it by myself."

"You could. But you don't have to."

She licks her lips. "Do you remember that one time when I was twenty and supposed to go out with Monica, but when I got to the house, she had already left for a date with Rich? There was a lot of miscommunication, and you were there for something. I forget what."

"I was fixing my parents' sink," I reply, remembering that night vividly. "And you were so disappointed that Monica had left, so we hung out."

"And you kissed me."

Hell, yes, I'd kissed her. She was so sweet and pretty.

"And you put on the brakes. Said Monica would kill you. And I came to my senses because you're almost ten years younger than me."

She nods, remembering that night.

"I had such a horrible, painful crush on you," she admits softly.

I knew. Of course, I knew. From the time she was in middle school, Tash watched me with lovesick eyes.

"But then we grew up," I add. "And you started dating Jeff Slimeball."

"Jeff Simpson," she says with a laugh. "He wasn't a slimeball. A little weird, maybe. He moved to Seattle. Last I heard, he and his husband are quite happy together."

"Good for him." I lean closer to her. "You have a little something right here."

I brush the tip of my finger over the corner of her mouth. Of course, I lied. There's nothing there.

But I want to touch her so badly I ache with it.

"What was it?" she asks quietly.

"Nothing." Her eyes narrow, but I only chuckle. "Your skin is so soft."

"That's what you said when I was twenty."

I swallow and watch her lips move. "I want to be clear here, Tash. I'm attracted to you, though not because of the situation we're currently in. I want to set that straight right now."

"So noted. And appreciated."

She watches as I lean in closer. I want to kiss her. I *need* to kiss her.

With the very tips of my fingers, I brush her dark locks off her cheek and over the soft crook of her ear.

She swallows and licks her lips.

Just as I'm about to lay my lips on hers, we hear, "Can I have some water?"

I sigh and glance to the right. Kelsey, looking tousled from sleep, holds her brown bear close to her chest.

"I'm thirsty," she says.

"Sure, sweetie," Tash says and stands from the couch. "And then right back to bed, okay?"

"Uh-huh," Kelsey murmurs as she follows Tash to the kitchen.

I blow out a breath and rub my hands over my face.

What am I doing? Getting tangled up with Tash only adds more complications to the whole situation.

I need to keep my hands—and my lips—to myself.

I'm about to say just that when I hear the woman walking back down the hall toward me.

"You know, I was just thinking—"

Before I can finish the thought, she straddles my lap.

I have no choice but to cup that gorgeous ass of hers in my hands—finally!—and stare up at her, waiting.

"Don't think," she advises.

CHAPTER 3

~NATASHA~

*S*am's hands grip my ass, those strong fingertips pressing firmly into the flesh beneath the denim of my jeans, and everything in me goes soft and just plain…wanton.

I'm crazy. I just straddled Sam as if I do it every day.

I'd *like* to do it every day.

I've wanted him for as long as I can remember, damn it, and he literally just admitted that he wants me, too.

So why *shouldn't* I get a little forward and enjoy him? Push some of the doubt, sadness, and goddamn *fear* out of my mind—if only for a little while.

"You're so fucking sweet," he whispers, and that's all it takes for my lips to descend on his. His hands grip me tighter as I wrap my arms around his shoulders and sink into him. And that's exactly what it feels like: a slow, delicious sinking into something so soft, warm, tender, and familiar that it tugs at my heart and turns me on all at the same time.

I move to push my hand through his messy blond hair, but my hand suddenly sings out in pain, making me gasp.

"What's wrong?" he asks, gasping for breath himself.

"Ouch." I frown as reality starts to settle in. "Damn hand."

"What the hell is wrong with me?" He doesn't nudge me off his lap, he simply lifts me, shifting until I'm cradled on his lap, my head resting on his shoulder. "I'm sorry."

"I'm not." I grin and shift my gaze from my throbbing hand to Sam's bright blue gaze. "I've wanted to kiss you for my whole life. And just like you said a little bit ago, it has nothing at all to do with the situation we presently find ourselves in. I just thought you weren't interested."

"I don't want to hurt your feelings," he admits with a sigh.

I raise a brow. "But?"

"It's not that I've never been interested in you," he begins and pauses to kiss my forehead. "But you were my baby sister's best friend. Significantly younger than me. It would have been damn creepy if I'd been into you."

"I'm not a baby now."

"No. You're a grown woman. And trust me, I've

noticed. But I'm not going to scoop you up and haul you off to bed when you're injured."

"It's only my hand," I remind him. "It's not my vagina."

He snorts. "Well, I'm relieved to hear that, but you're still uncomfortable. And the kids are here."

"Yeah, I can't argue that point." I let myself lean on him, just for a minute. Sam's always been tall and lean. He's only started to pack on the muscles over the past couple of years. He trained hard for his place in the fire department.

The hot body is a bonus.

"Can I interest you in a date?" he asks, surprising me.

"What kind of date?"

"A real one." He chuckles. "Noah offered to watch the kids. They'll have fun at the sanctuary, and I can take you out for a meal that you don't have to cook. With no one around that you have to cut up food for."

"I mean, if you need help, I've become quite the food chopper recently."

His lips twitch. "What do you say?"

"Sure." I nod and lean on him again. "I'd like that. Thanks for asking me."

"Thanks for saying yes."

"Auntie Tash?"

I sigh and glance over to where Kelsey is standing by the hallway.

"Yes, baby?"

"I had a bad dream." Her big blue eyes, so much like Sam's, well with big crocodile tears, and I open my arms for her to come sit with us.

"Come on, sweetie. Come sit with us. It's okay."

"Did you have a bad dream, too?" she asks me once she's settled on both of our laps.

"Why do you ask?"

"Because Uncle Sam is holding you like you had a bad dream."

"Oh." I smile and brush her soft blond hair off her cheek. "No. We were just talking, and I needed a cuddle. What was your bad dream about?"

She nuzzles closer to me and tucks her head under my chin, but she doesn't answer me. I let her sit for a long moment and then kiss her sweet little head.

"Don't want to talk about it?"

She shakes her head.

"Is it the same one you've been having?"

She nods.

"I'm sorry, honey. We can snuggle until you're ready to go back to bed."

"Can I sleep wif you?"

She turns those big eyes up to me. I know I'm being had. She's laying it on thick.

But how can anyone ever say no to that face?

"You sleep better in your bed," I remind her. "But I guess you can sleep in mine."

"Okay."

"Let's go. I'll tuck you in, and then I'm going to talk to Uncle Sam some more."

She hops off my bed and happily jogs down the hall to my bedroom.

"Sorry," I mutter as I slide off Sam's lap. "You don't have to stay. It's getting late."

"I can stay until after she's in bed," he offers. "I'll tuck her in."

He stands and kisses me on the forehead, then walks past me and down the hall.

I hear the murmur of his voice, although I can't hear what he says as he tucks his niece into my bed.

I curl up in the corner of the couch again and wince as I hug my injured hand to my chest.

It aches like a son of a bitch. I hope it heals quickly because there's no way I can do everything that needs to be done with it injured like this. I have laundry to do, dishes to wash, bathrooms to clean, and a million other chores that require both hands.

"Why are you scowling?" Sam asks when he returns.

"Oh, I'm just brooding. I guess it's good that I'm not working right now. There's no way I could do nails with my hand like this."

"Are you going to be okay?"

"Of course. It'll heal. I'll make do. The kids will just have to help me a little more than usual, but I'll make it a game for them. It'll be fine."

"Should I stay here for a few days until the worst of

it is over?" he asks as he sits next to me. "It's not a problem."

"I had to stash all of my nail stuff in the third bedroom," I reply, shaking my head. "It's packed full because I literally just threw it all in there since the twins wanted to share a room, and—"

"Take a breath," he suggests with a laugh. "I'm fine on the couch. Trust me, I've slept on far worse."

"Aren't you working this week?"

"On call," he says with a shrug. "If I get called, I'll go. I don't have to sit at the station twenty-four-seven. It'll just be for a few days, while you heal up a bit."

"If you're offering, I'm accepting. But please don't feel like you *have* to."

"I rarely do anything I don't want to do," he says. "I'll go home tonight, grab a few things, and come back tomorrow morning."

"Oh, good. Because tomorrow is the first day of... well, shit."

"First day of kindergarten."

"How did I forget? Crap, Sam. I have to get some things done tonight. Monica bought these little chalkboards to write in cute things for first-day pictures. I need to make sure their new outfits are washed and ready, and I have to make their lunches."

"Okay, change of plans. I'll head home and grab some stuff and then come back here to help you."

"You really don't have to do that."

"Sure, I do. It's their first day of school." He winks and grabs his keys. "I'll be back in an hour."

BY THE TIME Sam makes it back to my house, all I've managed to do is set out the kids' clothes for the morning. Thank God, I washed them last week.

"How's it going?" he asks when he walks in.

"I'm moving slow," I admit. "This stupid hand aches like crazy."

"Take some of the damn medicine."

His voice is firm and leaves no room for argument.

"I'm here. If anything happens and you're out cold, it's handled. Take it, Tash."

"Yeah, okay." I don't even bother arguing because I know he's right, and I'm in a decent amount of pain.

"Just point and tell me what to do. I'm pretty handy."

He waits as I swallow the pill with a glass of water and then open the fridge.

"Okay, I was just going to make them sandwiches and slice up some apples. I have these little individual peanut butter cups for them to dip their apples in." Sam and I get to work building their lunches. I do a lot of pointing and doling out instructions, and he moves quickly, keeping up with me easily.

Once the bags are packed, Sam opens a little bag of Cheetos and digs in.

"Those are for the kids," I remind him.

"Quality control," he says with a wink and munches happily. "Okay, now what?"

"I have these chalkboards," I say and walk to the closet where I stowed them. "We have to fill in these blanks."

"How do we know how tall they are?" he asks and blinks at me.

"I started measuring them," I answer and show him the place on the pantry doorjamb where I've made marks with a pencil, noting the name and date next to it. "We'll use the most recent one. They've grown more than an inch in the past couple of months."

"They grow like weeds," he says.

"We'll have to fill out some of this in the morning because I forgot to ask them the questions. Like, what they want to be when they grow up."

"You'll have to write it. I have horrible chicken scratch."

"My right hand is injured."

"So?"

"I'm *right-handed.*"

His eyes go wide, and then he cringes. "Okay, we'll make it work."

I yawn and glance at the clock. "I think we have it handled. I'm going to bed. Let me grab you some linens for the couch. Actually, you can go home and just come back in the morning if you want."

"I'll sack out here. No sense going home for just a

few hours, only to turn around and come back. Besides, I hate my rental. It's full of wall-to-wall boxes between my stuff and Monica's. It's not homey like this."

"I'm sorry." I shake my head when he narrows his eyes at me. "I know, you don't want or need my apology, but I'm sorry anyway. That you had to pass on the other job, right after you sold your house. And that you had to hurry up and rent something else. It's just a big mess."

"I didn't pass on the job," he says, surprising me.

"What? But you're still here."

"Of course, I am." He runs his hand through his hair and pitches the empty chip bag into the trash. "Like you said, it's been a mess. I don't know what's going to happen, or how it'll all shake out, but they held the job for me for six months."

"Oh." I swallow the lump in my throat. I thought that with us co-parenting the kids, Sam would have passed on the job.

Does this mean he'll take off in a few months to live a new life in Spokane, leaving me here with the kids?

He could.

And it sounds like he might.

"Like I said, I don't know what'll happen. But I didn't want to close that door completely."

"Sure." I nod and offer him a fake smile. "I get it. I'm headed to bed. There are extra blankets and pillows in the hall linen closet."

"Are you okay?"

"Of course. Just tired as always, these days. And the medicine is probably kicking in. I'll see you in the morning."

I hurry out of the kitchen and make a beeline for my bedroom. I never shut my door all the way because I want to be able to hear the kids.

But I want to tonight. I want to close it and have a good cry. If Sam leaves town for that job, I'll lose one more person who means something to me. Maybe not permanently, but if he doesn't live here, it won't be the same.

It's another thing to grieve.

And I've had my fill of grief—enough to last a decade.

It takes me longer than usual to change into a nightgown because of my sore hand, and when I finally get into bed, I discover that Kelsey has managed to angle herself over the entire King-sized mattress.

How that's possible, I have no idea.

I nudge her over to the side and slip between the sheets. Thanks to the medicine, my eyes are heavy, and my brain is foggy. I've just turned over to drift off when a little arm slips around mine, and Kelsey rests her head against my shoulder.

"Night, Mama."

My eyes open, and I stare at the ceiling for what feels like an hour.

I know she's asleep and didn't know what she was saying. She won't remember it tomorrow.

But man, it breaks my heart.

I miss your mama, I think to myself. I miss her so very much.

"SHH, Uncle Sam said not to wake her up."

"But we have to. We have to go to school."

I wait just a heartbeat and then sit up really fast and yell, "Boo!"

The twins giggle, and Kevin jumps up onto the bed with me, bouncing a couple of times.

"You're already dressed." I frown at them both. "And your hair is combed."

"Uncle Sam helped," Kelsey says. "He said we should be quiet and let you sleep because of your hand. Does it still hurt?"

Like a bitch.

"Yeah, a little."

"You didn't follow orders," Sam accuses as he marches into the room. "I turned my back for twenty seconds."

"It's okay." I tousle my hair with my hands. "I have to get up. I don't want to miss the first day of school."

"We have donuts," Kevin announces as he jumps off the bed. "I want another one!"

"That explains the energy level," I say dryly as

Kelsey follows her brother out of my room. "You took them for donuts?"

"No, I got up before everyone else, so I went and got a dozen. There's plenty left for you, as long as we don't leave the kids to their own devices for too long. I'll let you get dressed into something more decent."

I scowl and look down. "It's a nightgown. I'm not showing anything."

Sam rubs his hand over his lips and then leans in to whisper in my ear. "I can see your nipples pressed against the cotton of that thing. And it makes me want things, Tash, that aren't appropriate with two five-year-olds waiting to go to school."

Without another word or touch, he turns and leaves the room.

Leaving me all hot and bothered. Damn him.

"It's just a simple cotton nightgown," I grumble. "It's not like I'm wearing something from Victoria's Secret or anything."

Still, I wiggle my way into leggings and a T-shirt with a blue flannel shirt over it, teasing my hair into a ponytail. I only wince a little when the motion makes my hand sing in protest.

"We're ready for pictures," Kevin announces, holding up his chalkboard. Every slot is filled in on both of them, and I turn my eyes to Sam.

"You filled them out."

"Yeah," he says with a nod. "I guess they didn't come out too bad."

"They look great." The writing isn't fancy like Monica's would have been, but the letters are perfectly legible. I can tell he put a lot of effort into this. "Thanks."

"Let's go outside for some pictures," Sam suggests.

The kids pose with their chalkboards on the porch, their little backpacks slung over their shoulders and wide smiles on their faces. I pose them together and separate.

And then we pile into the truck and head the short distance to the elementary school.

"We'll be here to get you when you're done," I remind them as we walk hand-in-hand to their class-room. We visited last week so they could meet their teacher and see the room they'll be in. We all thought it was a good idea for them to be in the same classroom this year as the twins tend to act out when they're on their own.

"Okay," Kevin says and doesn't even bother to wave at us as he hurries off to see his friends.

"I don't want to," Kelsey says and turns to me with tears in her eyes. "I want to go with you."

"You've been looking forward to school," I remind her gently and squat next to her. "There's your friend, Trinity. And Lucy. You know the other kids, Kels."

She grabs my leg, but Mrs. Delgado hurries over with a wide, welcoming smile on her pretty face.

"Hi there, Kelsey. Welcome. I'm so excited you're here. We're going to have such a fun day."

47

"I love you, and I'll see you very soon." I kiss her cheek, and Mrs. Delgado seamlessly takes the little girl's hand and leads her away, giving me the nod to go.

Sam and I leave the classroom and walk out to his truck.

But when we climb inside, he doesn't start the engine.

"It should be Monica," I say and wipe away a tear. "Monica should be here to take her babies to school, take pictures, and fill out their chalkboards."

"I know it." Sam sighs. "But the thing is, Tash, she's not. She's not here. No matter how unfair it is. You can't feel guilty every time there's a new life event in the kids' lives over the next thirty years because there will be dozens of them."

"I know." I wipe my nose on the handkerchief he offers me. "I know that. But, Jesus, Sam, it's only been a few months. I'm still adjusting to this. Monica was excited for today. She prepared for it *months* ago. She should be here to see it. It pisses me off that she isn't."

"Me, too, honey. Me, too." He kisses my hand. "Rich and my sister were good parents. They waited a long time to have kids, and they loved it. All we can do is make them proud of us. And of the kids."

"Yeah." I swallow the last of my tears. "You're right. I think I need a donut."

"Coming right up."

CHAPTER 4

~ SAM ~

"I see Isha!" Kelsey exclaims, pointing at Noah and Fallon's daughter playing in a field with puppies. "Can I go?"

"Go ahead," Tash says with a smile. "Have fun. Try not to get too dirty."

"We're at a ranch," I remind her as we glance around the Lazy K Ranch, owned by the King family, outside of Cunningham Falls. I've been here plenty over the years, from helping with medical emergencies to enjoying barbecues like this one. "They're gonna get dirty."

"I know, but I have to make an effort to keep them clean." She grins and looks around. "There must be a hundred people here. Maybe more."

"And you know them all, so don't get shy on me now."

"I'm not shy. I'm surprised. I haven't been to a King BBQ in many years. They've grown."

She's not wrong.

As the kids married and had children of their own, along with making new friends in town, the parties have gone from smallish get-togethers of a few dozen people to huge events with big white tents and rented tables and chairs.

And with this being the end of summer, it looks like the whole town made a point to show up.

"There you are," Cara King, one of the owner's wives says as she approaches with a big smile. "As you can see, we have a zoo going on here. I've been told a fishing party is getting ready to walk to the creek out back. I stay away from there."

She winks at me, and I immediately remember that early summer day all those years ago when she and her nephew, Seth, got into trouble in the creek.

"We have food over that way," she continues and points to the tent surrounded by mosquito netting. "Drinks are in there, too. In the field over there, we have a friendly game of horseshoes and cornhole. Zack and Josh have been swearing at each other all day, so enter at your own risk. Make yourselves at home. Let me know if you need anything."

"Thanks, Cara," Tash says. "I think you're going to need help with cleanup when all of this is over."

"I outsourced this year." Cara winks. "Have fun, guys."

She strolls away to welcome others who just arrived, and Noah and Fallon walk our way, holding out cold drinks to us.

"You look like you could use this," Noah says as he passes me a beer.

"Thanks."

"I see the kids found the puppies," Fallon says with a grin and rubs her round, pregnant belly. "Isha is *not* talking me into one."

"No, ma'am." Noah winks at her. "No way."

"I'm serious, Noah King." Fallon frowns. "I have enough to do. Puppy training is not on that list."

"Let's get out of the sun," Tash suggests, and we walk over to some Adirondack chairs set under a pair of umbrellas.

"What happened to your hand?" Fallon asks her.

"Oh, I had a run-in with a knife a few days ago. It's not as bad as it was." We all sit and enjoy watching the people around us; then she points at a group of teenagers hanging out by the above-ground swimming pool. "Who is that?"

"Miles, Sarah, Layla, and Kimberly," Noah says, pointing at the teenagers. "Miles and Sarah are Zack's twins. Layla's Ty and Lauren's daughter, and Kim is Cara and Josh's daughter. They're all in the same age range and attached at the hip."

"Who's the dude draped all over Layla?" I ask, narrowing my eyes.

"New kid in town," Fallon says. "And that makes

him mysterious and *incredibly* attractive to sixteen-year-old girls."

"And what does her daddy have to say about that?" I ask.

"Her daddy isn't happy." I glance up to find Ty standing nearby, watching the kids with the eyes of a protective father. Ty's a successful attorney here in Cunningham Falls, but he's not in a suit today. He's in a Megadeth T-shirt, his sleeve of tattoos showing. And as the boy in question leans in to plant his lips on Layla's cheek, Ty's jaw clenches. "Little son of a bitch better watch himself."

"We could kill him," Josh says as he and Zack join us. "There're plenty of places to dispose of the body on the ranch. No one will find him."

"Let's not rush into homicide," Ty says but crosses his arms over his chest when the boy pats Layla's ass as she stands to walk to the drink tent. "Layla, come here."

Her smile dims as she approaches her dad. "Yeah?"

"Let him touch you like that again, and I'll take his hand off."

Layla rolls her eyes. "It was harmless."

"Like hell," Ty growls. "I've been that kid's age. It wasn't harmless."

"Fine." She stomps away, her red hair flying as she flips it over her shoulder.

"I want my baby back," Ty says with a sigh. "And she reminds me every day that that's never gonna happen."

"At least, she's not pregnant," Zack says with a

helpful smile, and Ty turns to pull Zack into a head-lock, only to end up on his back in the dirt.

"Men are violent," Tash says, sipping her hard seltzer.

"Hey, what's going on?" Seth King, Zack's eldest son, says as he jumps into the mix, hurling himself on his dad's back.

"Oof," Zack says, under the weight of his adult son. "Get the fuck off me, kid."

The jumble of pure male testosterone untangles itself, and the three men grin at each other, heaving in breaths.

"You may be twenty-eight," Zack says to his son, "but I can still take you."

"In your dreams, old man." Seth turns to me with a grin. "Hey, Sam."

"Hey, yourself. Stay away from the creek today, okay? No more broken ankles."

"I'm never gonna live that down," Seth says and shakes his head. "Trust me, Aunt Cara would kill me if I tried a stunt like that again. So, I just learned not to tell her."

"How are things in the park?" I ask him. Seth's been a ranger up in Glacier National Park for several years. He has a degree in wildlife biology and loves the park and the animals.

"Busy. Busiest summer to date for tourist traffic. Had an idiot put a bear cub in his car to *warm it up*." He snarls in disgust. "Asshole. We aren't a petting zoo. Anyway, it's good. Oh, wait a sec."

He looks over the crowd and then whistles and gestures for someone to join us.

"Tash, Gage is here," Seth says to a surprised Natasha. "He just got to town."

Natasha's eyes go wide as her brother joins us. Gage offers his sister a small smile.

"Hey."

"Hi." She stands, and they embrace in the most awkward hug of all time before she steps back and tucks her hair behind her ear. "Back in town, huh?"

"Yeah, just got here last week. I meant to call, but I got busy. You know how it is."

"Right." She nods once. "I know how it is. Glad you're here safely."

"You know, if you ever want to have dinner with the parents—"

"I don't," she cuts him off. "But tell them hi for me."

She sits down once more and sips her drink. Gage shrugs.

"Sure. I'll tell them."

"Welcome home," I say. Gage is in the Army and has been God knows where for the past few years. He's also Seth's best friend.

I should have known he'd be here today.

I don't know the story behind the tension between Tash and the rest of her family, but I'll be asking about it later.

Now isn't the time or place.

"I think I'll go harass Layla's new boyfriend," Seth says with a grin. "He looks way too comfortable over there."

"Good boy," Zack says as Seth and Gage saunter over to the pool, pull off their shirts, and sit right next to Layla.

"Here's hoping they scare the little asshole off," Ty mutters. "I'm gonna go find my wife."

He stalks off.

"Speaking of wives," Zack says. "Mine will kill me if I don't check the list she gave me this morning."

Zack hurries off, and then Josh's parents call him away.

When it's just the four of us, Fallon turns to Natasha.

"If you ever want to talk about it, I'm a good listener."

Tash glances at Fallon and taps her can to the other woman's water. "I'm good. But thanks."

"Mom! Mom!" Isha comes running and flings herself into Fallon's lap, having no regard whatsoever for the belly between them. "Can Kevin and Kelsey come to our house tonight? We could have a sleepover and everything."

Isha grips Fallon's face in her little hands and presses her nose to her mother's.

"Pweeeeeease?"

"It's a long weekend," Noah says and glances at me. "Fine with us, if it is with you."

"If you're sure," Tash says. "They're a handful, and—"

"It'll be great," Fallon assures Tash easily. "Don't even worry about it. We'll bring them home Monday afternoon."

"Wait, you're going to take them for the rest of the *weekend*?" Tash asks.

"Sure. It'll be fun."

"Yay!" Isha exclaims and hurries off her mother's lap so she can go tell the others.

"If you need or want to bring them home early, it's no problem," Tash assures Fallon.

"Stop worrying." Fallon pats Tash's shoulder. "We've got this."

"I guess this means we can have a date night." I waggle my eyebrows at Natasha. "You in?"

"Sure. I'm in."

"Oh my God, I ate too much bread." Tash sits back in her seat and pats her flat stomach. "I have a food baby."

"Worth it, though," I say as I polish off my tiramisu. I brought her to Ciao for dinner, one of her favorite places. We walked here from her house, anticipating eating all the carbs in the world and needing a walk afterward.

"No one approached us today. Not even at the BBQ."

I set my green napkin on the table and nod. "You're right. Is that good or bad?"

"It's good, I think." She eyes the last piece of garlic bread in the basket. "I mean, I was sick of it, and it drove me nuts, so it's a good thing."

"But?"

"But does it mean that people are forgetting them?"

"You're an overthinker, Natasha Mills."

"Yeah." She shrugs and reaches for the bread, then bites into it. "I always have been. This dinner was a nice surprise. Thanks."

"You're welcome." I sit back and watch her, feeling something stir inside me when she licks her bottom lip. "That dress is nice on you."

"Oh, thanks." She glances down as if she doesn't remember what she's wearing.

But I'll never forget it.

A pink sundress with thin little straps on the shoulders. No bra straps.

This is the second time in only a few days that the thought of Natasha's bare breasts has gotten me all hot and bothered.

"Sam?"

"Yeah?"

"I asked if you were ready to head out."

"Oh, sure." I stand and offer my hand to help her

out of the booth. When she walks ahead of me, I keep my hand on the small of her back.

I like touching her—more than I thought I would.

She could become addicting.

I haven't decided how I feel about that, exactly.

Tash takes a deep breath and lifts her face to the sky. "It's such a nice day. I'm glad we walked."

"Me, too. I need to walk off the tiramisu." I slip my hand into hers as we stroll along the sidewalk, through the heart of downtown Cunningham Falls. Mrs. Blakely steps out of Little Deli to pull her sign in for the night and sees us, her gaze immediately falling to our clasped hands.

But she doesn't say anything. She just winks and walks back into her shop, locking the door behind her.

"Interesting," Tash murmurs and looks up at me. "Did you say something to her?"

"Nope." I laugh when she stares up at me, daring me to lie to her. "I promise. Maybe she just learned her lesson."

"Maybe."

It's late into the evening now, but the sky still hangs onto a bit of light, and the birds sing in the trees as we make our way through town.

Tash lives in an older house in one of the first neighborhoods established in Cunningham Falls. If I remember correctly, I think she's renting from Ty Sullivan.

But that's not what I want to discuss with her tonight.

"Tell me about Gage." Her hand immediately stiffens in mine, but I hold strong.

"We're just not close."

"Bullshit." It's not said with force or anger, just conversationally.

"I don't know him," she finally says with a sigh. "Gage and I haven't been close since we were little. And once he went into the Army, we drifted apart. We stayed in touch for a while, but it didn't last long."

"Why not?"

She blows out a breath. "You're damn nosy."

"Curious."

"My parents and I do *not* get along. At all. Thankfully, they don't live here anymore. They moved to Hawaii because my dad's sister got a teaching job there, and my parents decided that island life was for them. And, to be honest, I don't miss them a whole lot."

"I thought they were dead." I frown. "Since you never talk about them, and I don't see them around town, I just figured they were no longer with us."

"They're alive and well, last I heard. I don't think I've spoken to my mom in about eight years. I talked to my dad a few weeks ago when he called to give his condolences about Monica. When I told him I'd be raising the kids—with you, of course—he just said, *'Good luck with that.'* Not, *'Can we help in any way?'* Or *'Do you need anything?'* So, there's no love lost there."

59

"What started it?" I ask.

"I went to nail school."

I blink down at her, certain I heard her wrong. "What?"

"Yep. They'd saved up a bunch of money over the years for me to go to college. I didn't need even a quarter of it for my schooling. I wanted to do nails. They accused me of choosing something cheap, so I could pocket the rest of the money."

"What the hell?"

"I know, right? The best part is, I didn't use *any* of it. Not even for school. I paid it off myself because I'd be damned if I used anything from them."

"Where did they want you to go to school?"

"Oh, they absolutely expected me to go to the University of Montana, just like they did. They're alumni. Dedicated doesn't even *begin* to describe their love for their alma mater."

"You seriously don't speak to your parents because you didn't go to the college they wanted you to?"

"No, *they* don't speak to *me.* And Gage has had a rough row with them as well because he went into the Army. But, in the beginning, he sided with them. He thought I should just shut up and go. He's not even a full year younger than me. And when it came time for his turn, he wanted the Army."

"I bet they weren't happy about that, either."

"Actually, they were thrilled. They said that if he wasn't going to their precious university, at least he would be doing something noble with his life, unlike his white-trash sister."

I stop on the sidewalk, just a block from Tash's house, and stare down at her in disbelief.

"You're fucking kidding me."

"I wish I were."

Anger, pure and ripe, fills me on her behalf. I want to beat the shit out of them for *ever* making her feel less than. Tash has done amazing things with her life and for her community.

"Shame on them," is all I can say.

"Absolutely."

We fall into step once more, and I follow her up the steps to her front door. Once she unlocks it, I cage her against the doorway.

She licks her lips, and I know that I'm a goner. Jesus, I want to kiss her more than I've ever wanted anything in my life.

So, I lower my face to hers. I brush her nose with mine and then sink into her, soaking her in. She moans and melts under me as my mouth opens, and I take my fill until I have to pull back and stare down at her.

Her brown eyes are heavy and full of lust as she gazes up at me.

"Sam?"

"Uh-huh."

"I think you should come inside."

"Good idea."

Once through the door, Tash's purse hits the floor. I

shut the door and round on her. I'm not nearly as gentle as I planned to be when I yank her against me and retake her mouth, spinning her and pressing her back against the door.

"So sweet," I whisper against her neck as I lick my way down her throat. I pull one of the straps of her dress to the side and nip her shoulder. "Jesus, Tash, I want you."

"Thank God, because if you'd said we shouldn't and left, I might have killed you dead."

I pull back to grin down at her. "Violent, aren't you?"

"Turned on, Sam. I'm damn turned on."

She slips the other strap down her arm, and the fabric pools around her waist, exposing her perfect breasts. The nipples are hard, and her chest heaves as she pants. I know in my gut that I couldn't walk out of here if the place were on fire.

"I'm not leaving," I promise.

"Good."

"And you're not going to wear clothes for about the next thirty-six hours."

"I can live with that."

CHAPTER 5

~NATASHA~

*I*s it the stress? The fact that Sam and I spend so much time together now that we have the kids to raise? Could it be because I've wanted him for as long as I can remember, and he's finally stripping me naked and having his wanton way with me?

I don't know what the reason is—and frankly, my brain is too mushy to really care. All I know for sure is that I need this.

I need *Sam.*

"Need you, too," he whispers before nibbling on my collarbone. I didn't even realize I'd said the words out loud.

If I weren't so incredibly turned on, I'd be embarrassed.

"Jesus, you're bare under this thing."

I grin and then gasp when he tugs my nipple right into his mouth and pulls.

Hard.

Christ, if I'd known that sex with Sam would be this *crazy*, I would have jumped him years ago.

He palms my ass with his big hands and turns to carry me to the bedroom.

"Need to see you," he growls, moving fast through the house. I fall onto the bed, my sandals slipping right off my feet as Sam yanks my dress down and tosses it on the floor.

"Holy fuck." He just stands there, staring down at me, and wipes the back of his hand over his mouth.

Suddenly shy, I move to cover my breasts, but he swiftly crawls over me and gently tugs my arm away, kissing my injured hand in the process.

"No. Don't cover yourself, Tash."

"You're just staring at me."

"Well, yeah. Of course, I am. You're so damn beautiful it hurts."

I grin again. "Aww, I bet you say that to all the girls, Sam Waters."

"No." He kisses me so gently, his lips a mere touch. "No, Natasha Mills, I don't."

His attention is gentle. Feather-light. It sends chills over my naked body as he barely brushes his fingertips down the center of my chest to my navel. When he licks the shell of my ear, I gasp.

He's *barely* touching me, and I'm ready to come out

of my skin.

"Let's get this show on the road." The words are rough, my voice thick with lust, but Sam just chuckles in my ear.

"We're on the road," he says. "But we're not getting in the fast lane this time."

"Let's not hang out in the slow lane, either."

I feel him smile against my skin. "Do you have any idea how long I've waited to get you here, in this exact spot, Tash?"

"Ditto. But damn it, Sam, I'm in knots here. If I don't have an orgasm *stat*, I'm going to come unglued—and not in a fun way. In a frustrated way. And neither of us wants that."

"You're right." He leans up and nods grimly. "That would be awful."

"Maybe the worst thing *ever*."

"We can't let that happen."

"Great."

I move to spread my legs, but he doesn't get undressed to do me. No, that would be too *normal* for Sam Waters.

He's never been predictable.

This man, this glorious, wonderful man, proceeds to scoot down the bed, and with his hands planted on both of my inner thighs to spread me, he face-plants right into the promised land.

"Sam!"

I almost jackknife into a sitting position, but then

his tongue gets busy, and all I can do is fist the bed linens and hold on for the ride of my life.

If this isn't the fast lane, I might want to rethink going into that lane because it could very well kill me dead.

His hands no longer hold me down. Instead, he brushes his fingers up and down the skin of my thighs, making me clench and squirm. When his tongue slips through my folds and inside me, I see stars.

Shooting stars.

Explosive, shooting stars.

I come apart as I cry out, gripping Sam's hair as I ride the delicious wave of ecstasy.

When the clouds part, Sam leisurely kisses his way up my stomach. When he reaches my breasts, he camps out and pays attention.

"For such a willowy woman, you have great boobs."

"Ha-ha. Funny."

"Not funny at all. True." He licks a nipple and then blows on it, watching in fascination as it hardens. "Sexy."

"Are we back in the slow lane?"

"Just for a minute," he says.

I blink.

"You're naked."

"So are you."

"I mean you weren't naked just a few minutes ago. When did that happen? Are you a wizard or something, who just magically strips off his clothes?"

"Yes."

I stare at him, and he laughs.

"You were busy enjoying your orgasm when I took them off."

"I didn't get to look at you."

He quirks an eyebrow, and with mischief in his eyes, he stands up and turns in a circle. "Better?"

"Hmm. Turn around again."

He does as I ask, and I admire his backside. Jesus, Mary, and Joseph, the man has an ass to write home about. And his back muscles!

He starts to turn back around, but I just say, "Stop."

"Do I have something stuck to my ass?"

"No, I'm just admiring it." I sit up and scoot over so I can bite the flesh of his butt. "And we need to talk about your back."

"What's wrong with it?"

"Absolutely nothing at all. The muscle tone is crazy, Sam."

"All the better to carry you with." He turns, and I'm eye-level with his *very* impressive dick. I reach for it and look up to find his eyes narrowing as he watches me intently.

"Hi there." I kiss the tip, the same way he did my nipples, and then blow on it.

"*Natasha.*"

"Oh, *now* you want to get in the fast lane?"

He laughs and tumbles me back onto the bed, then covers me. With those deep blue eyes trained on mine, he sheaths his cock, slides right inside and seats himself, balls-deep.

"Oh, damn."

Tears threaten. Not because he hurt me or made me do anything I didn't want to do. No, it's because I've waited *years* for this. For *him*. I'm no virgin, but deep down, I always yearned for Sam.

And here he is.

Inside me.

And looking at me as if I'm the sexiest thing he's ever seen in his life.

"You okay?"

"Oh, yeah."

"Then why do I see tears swimming in those gorgeous eyes?" He kisses my cheek and brushes his fingers through my hair.

"I'm not crying."

"Okay."

I hitch my legs up higher on his hips, and he takes a long, deep breath.

"Sam?"

"Right here, babe."

"Holy shit, Sam."

His lips tip up into a sweet smile. "Yeah, that's what I was thinking. Now, fast lane or slow? It's up to you."

"I'm not the only one here."

"You're the most important one."

And just like that, I might have tipped over into love

with this man. *Real* love, not the crush I've had for most of my life.

I knew he was special.

I didn't know he was *this* incredible.

"Maybe the middle lane?"

He rubs his nose over mine and sets a rhythm, a push and pull that's right there in the middle. Not too slow, not too fast. Just perfect so he hits all the right spots but ensures I don't finish too quickly.

He takes my good hand, kisses it, and then traps it over my head against the mattress as he picks up speed, just a tiny bit.

"God, I can't hold back."

"Don't. Don't hold back with me."

His jaw clenches, and with a low growl, Sam loses himself. All I can do is watch with absolute female satisfaction as he comes apart.

When he pushes in, pulsing and rubbing against my clit, I follow him right over.

"Whoa." I swallow hard, and then he rolls us onto our sides so he can relax next to me. "Who knew it would be like that?"

"Me." He brushes a lock of my hair off my cheek. "I knew."

"Whatever."

"Do you feel okay? Do you need anything?"

"I'm perfectly happy right now, thanks for asking." His face is mere inches from mine as we both share my pillow. "Does this change everything?"

"No overthinking," he says gently. "But, yes. It changes everything."

"That's what I thought."

"Do I overthink every single thing?" I ask as I make myself at home in Aspen's kitchen, getting to work on my famous margaritas.

"If you've suddenly changed everything about your personality, then no." Aspen grins when I narrow my eyes at her.

"Don't say anything without us!" Her Royal Highness, Princess Eleanor—better known as our bestie, Ellie—says as she and Alice hurry into the room. "We got here as fast as we could."

"And by that she means that my husband drove as slow as possible," Alice adds with a grimace. "That man doesn't understand urgency unless someone has a gun pointed at Callum. Then, he picks up speed."

"Thankfully, the whole gun pointed at my husband thing doesn't happen often," Aspen says with a wink. "You haven't missed much yet. Tash was just asking if I think she's an overthinker."

"No, not at all." Ellie rolls her eyes. "Never. Not you."

"Sarcasm isn't dignified on royalty," I inform her.

I love these women. They're my tribe. Aspen owns Drips & Sips here in town and married Ellie's brother,

Prince Callum, several years ago. The royal family is deeply rooted here in Cunningham Falls now, but they bounce back and forth between Montana and the United Kingdom.

Alice is married to Callum's personal bodyguard, and she does most of the cooking for the royals. She's become a great friend since we met her back when Callum and Aspen were dating.

"I'm incredibly dignified when I'm sarcastic." Ellie sniffs regally, making me smile. "Why are you worried about overthinking?"

"Sam pointed it out, and I guess I never really gave it much thought before." I squeeze fresh limes into the blender.

"How are things with the kids and Sam?" Alice asks, the three of them sobering.

"Things with Sam are *really* good." I bite my lip, thinking about the weekend we just had. "We had sex."

Three gasps fill the kitchen.

"*Natasha*," Aspen breathes. "And you haven't told us yet?"

"I didn't see you before tonight."

"You *lead* with that information," Ellie says. "As soon as we walk through the door, the first words out of your mouth should be: '*I did the dirty with Sam.*'"

"It wasn't dirty." I add more lime and then pulse the blender. "Well, some parts were kind of dirty. But now, I have doubts."

"About the dirtiness?" Aspen asks.

"No, about Sam. It probably wasn't a good idea to have two sex-filled days with him."

"Where were the kids?"

"Noah and Fallon had them. I feel like I should send them flowers. Or dinner or something. Anyway, it was probably a mistake because now we have to raise two kids together. What if it's all weird?"

"Was it weird earlier today?" Alice wants to know.

I frown and take five glasses out of the cabinet. "No. But he hasn't been to the house since we had the incredible sex. He was on call, and there was a barn fire out by the King ranch. I guess it was a doozy. He worked on it for a long time. They lost some animals. It was a mess."

"So you haven't seen him to know if things are off," Aspen says.

"Right." I sigh and pour five glasses full of margaritas.

"Honey," Ellie says softly. "There are only four of us here."

"I know." I don't look up as I slide a glass over to an empty stool at the island. "But this is the first time we've had a margarita night since it happened, and I need to do this. Because she's here, you guys. She's still here with us."

"Of course, she is," Alice says with a forced smile and raises her glass. "To our precious Monica. Our sweet friend. May you be having a margarita in heaven."

"I'll drink to that," Aspen says and clinks her glass to ours. She offers me a sympathetic smile, and I can almost read her mind.

I know how hard this is. I'm right here if you need me.

Only Aspen would know exactly what I'm going through. She lost her first husband and daughter to a horrible accident years ago. And during everything that's happened over the past several months, Aspen's been my rock.

"I know you had other duties to see to," I say softly. "That you should have been in London, and instead you and Callum stayed here so you could help me out."

"I don't know what you're talking about," Aspen begins, but then softens when she sees the look on my face. "Honey, you needed help. Of course, we stayed. The kids love it here, we're safe here, and there's no reason I *can't* be here. The king and queen understood completely. Please don't think that being here for you was a hardship for us in any way."

"We're all here to help," Alice adds. "I'm happy to take the kids to play with mine anytime."

"Thank you." I sip my drink and sigh. "Right now, they're happy to be back in school. And so far, they haven't gotten into any trouble. Thank God. This summer, I was sure they were both headed for a life of crime."

"They're adjusting, too," Ellie says.

"Sometimes, if Kelsey has had a bad dream and wants to sleep with me, she'll call me *Mama* in her sleep." I swallow hard. "It just about kills me. Because I know she doesn't even realize she's doing it. It's just so *sad*, you know?"

"Heartbreaking," Aspen agrees.

"I see the salon sold," Ellie says. "Have you been in?"

"No." I shake my head and refill my glass, then open a bag of chips and fetch the guacamole out of Aspen's fridge. "No, I can't go in. I haven't gone since the day I went in to pack up my things."

"Not even when you sold it?" Alice asks.

"Not even then. But I hear Reagan's doing a good job with it, and that makes me happy."

"What are you going to do?" Aspen asks.

"About what?"

"About a job, Tash," she continues. "Now that things are settling down, and the kids are in school, I'm just wondering what you'll do next."

"I feel like I haven't had the brain space to think about it," I admit. "And then I hurt my hand, so I definitely couldn't go back to doing nails for a while. I don't know if I want to do nails again. It was something I did with Monica, and I don't think it would be as fun, you know?"

"Maybe a career change?" Alice asks.

"I need to do something. My savings will run out eventually."

"I'm quite sure there's a trust for the kids and the person caring for them," Aspen says with a frown.

"That money is theirs, not mine. It'll be there for them when they're adults."

"It's there for this very reason," Alice reminds me. "That in the case of...*this*, the caretakers can afford to care for the kids."

"I know, and if worse comes to worst, I'll use it. But I don't need it. It's for Kelsey and Kevin. I'll figure it out." I shrug and pop a chip into my mouth. "Enough about me. Let's talk about you guys."

"Oh, no," Ellie says, shaking her head slowly. "You're going to tell us more about this sexy time with Sam. You've had a crush on that man since before I met you, and I need to know every little detail."

"Yes." Aspen leans in. "I'm here for this content. Give us deets. Use all the naughty words, and don't leave anything out. If you forget something, you have to start over again at the beginning."

"You're all a bunch of perverts."

No one responds. They just stare at me, intently. Like I'm about to deliver the secrets of the universe.

"I mean...it was nice."

"If it was just *nice*, it was a waste of time," Aspen says. "But maybe it's none of our business."

That's exactly something that Monica would say.

"You guys." I sigh and stare dreamily out the window that gives us a killer view of the mountains. "He's so...*sweet*. And kind of bossy. And funny. Like the chemistry is ridiculous. And we just fit, you know?"

"Yeah." Ellie sighs, her face filled with romantic softness. "I do. It's the best feeling ever."

"And he's fun. It's not all stiff and boring and awkward. He can't get enough of my body, and I'm not even a little bit self-conscious because he's so into it. There's just no room to be unsure."

"That's the best," Aspen says with a nod. "The. Best."

"And then I asked him if everything would change. Or maybe I said, *'Does this change everything?'*, and he told me to stop overthinking. But then he said that it did change everything, and I don't really know what that means because all we did was bone for two days, and he's been fighting a fire and we haven't talked."

"Breathe," Alice advises. "Take a breath."

"Obviously, when he's no longer on call, you'll be able to chat," Ellie says. "And you're definitely over-thinking this. If the sex was that good and easy, there's nothing at all to worry about."

"But, the sex was easy for you and Liam, and you still had doubts," I remind her.

"Well, yes, because I too am an overthinker." She laughs and then shrugs. "But it worked out in the end. My advice to you is: don't make him travel all over the Earth to find you. Just be honest with him."

"I'll be honest." I finish my second margarita. "It would help if I was drunk."

"No." Aspen laughs and eats a chip. "No, it wouldn't."

CHAPTER 6

~SAM~

J've been tired before. You don't work the job I do with its demanding hours and the physical demands every day without the exhaustion that comes with it.

But this week has been a bitch and a half.

We lost a large barn and several outbuildings at the Blakely homestead. It was devastating for their farm. And it burned for days. Several of us stayed out there around the clock to ensure the fire didn't spread underground and head for the main house.

I'm exhausted and still filthy, despite a long shower at the station.

And I'm irritable.

The apartment I've been renting over the past several months is *not* home. I hate this place. It's just wall-to-wall boxes from floor to ceiling. Some of it is my stuff, other things are from Monica's house. I could shove it all into a storage unit, but I haven't had the time or the energy to deal with it.

I'm hardly here anyway.

I shuffle through several days-worth of mail, then toss it on the table and open the fridge. My stomach has been growling all day.

I have three beers from a six-pack I bought in May, a full container of brown matter that used to be guac, and half a pizza that I don't even remember buying.

"Shit."

I slam the door shut just as my phone rings.

"Waters."

"What are you doing?" Liam Cunningham has been my best friend since childhood. And because he's married to a princess, he's rarely in town these days. But they've been sticking close since the *accident*. I think both Liam and his wife Ellie, who is also one of Tash's closest friends, want to keep an eye on us.

"Staring into the abyss of my empty fridge."

"Fun times," he says good-naturedly.

"I hate this place. This apartment. Since I sold my house just before Mon—before she died, and I needed a place to park my ass, I took the first thing that came up. Rentals in this town are few and far between and cost a shit-ton of money. But this apartment isn't home. Being here depresses me."

"Where do you want to be?"

Natasha fills my mind, her sweet smile and cozy home. The kids with their giggles.

"Sam?"

"I should be at Tash's." I sit in my only chair and rub my eyes. "But I just got in from a seventy-two-hour shift, and I'm fucking exhausted."

"If you want to be with Tash, go be with her."

I frown. "You make it sound so easy, man."

"Why isn't it? Don't overthink it. If that's where you want to be, go. She'll welcome you there, and you know it."

"I always accuse her of being the overthinker."

I scratch my cheek, thinking it over. Then shake my head when I realize what I'm doing.

"Did you need something? Sorry, I just dumped all over you."

"I was just checking in. Let's do a beer night later this week. Ellie and I have to go to London for a while. We leave next Monday. I'd like to see you before we go."

"Consider it done. I'm in. But not here. It's not fit for company."

"I'll text you. Go hang out at Tash's. And get some rest."

"Thanks."

He hangs up, and I only have to think it over for about thirty seconds. He's right. I don't want to be here in this depressing mess of a place that is most certainly *not* my home.

So, I grab a bag, throw some clean clothes into it, and lock the place up behind me before climbing

KRISTEN PROBY

into my truck and driving across town to Tash's place.

It's been raining for the past twelve hours. The kind that settles in and lets you know it's going to stay for a while. We were due. It was a dry, hot summer, and we paid dearly for it with massive wildfires and our fair share of residential blazes, as well.

Montana needs the rain.

I park in front of Tash's house and leave my bag in the truck, just in case she kicks me out.

Not that I think she will, but I learned a long time ago not to take anything for granted when it comes to women.

Before I can even knock on the door, it swings open, and an excited Kevin grins up at me. "You're here!"

"I am. You shouldn't open the door like that."

"You're not a stranger," he points out and opens it wide so I can get inside. "You're Uncle Sam."

"True enough. Where are Tash and Kels?"

"In the kitchen, doing women stuff."

I cock a brow and ruffle his hair. "If your Aunt Tash hears you talk like that, she'll have your hide. Let's go find them."

"What's a hide?"

"Your skin."

"Yuck."

"Now, give that a stir. Just a light one. You don't want to send red sauce flying all over your stovetop."

Tash and Kelsey are looking down into a pot of sauce on the stove with Kelsey standing on a chair.

It's kind of adorable. I whip out my phone and snap a photo before they look my way.

"Uncle Sam is here," Kevin announces. "And he said you're going to take my skin off."

Tash turns and raises an eyebrow. "Well, what did you do?"

"Nothing." Kevin's grin is sly as he leans on his aunt. "I love you."

"Uh-huh. I love you, too. Hey there." She smiles up at me. "You look exhausted."

"It's been a long week."

"Well, you're just in time for dinner," she says. "We're making spaghetti, and that feeds an army, so I hope you're hungry."

"I'm starving, actually."

"Great." Her eyes narrow on me. "Kids, why don't you go watch some Scooby?"

"But I'm helping with the s'ghetti," Kelsey points out. "It's my job today."

"It just has to cook for a while," Tash replies. "Go ahead and take a break. I'll let you know when it's time to stir again."

The kids run for the living room, leaving us alone, so I pull her to me and kiss the hell out of her.

And just like that, I feel better.

"Hey," I whisper.

"Hi there." She leans her cheek on my chest. "I'm glad you came by. I was going to call you later."

"I tried to get time to call you, but that fire was a mess." I sigh and hug her close. "One of the worst I've seen."

"Is everyone okay?"

"The humans are," is all I'll say. She doesn't need to hear about what happened to the animals. "Lost some buildings and crops. It helped that it cooled down so much last night, and the rain started early this morning."

"I'm glad. Do you get a couple of days off now to rest?"

"Three," I confirm. "I plan to sleep at least one of those."

"I don't blame you. I'll get you fed so you can get home to bed." I frown, and she tilts her head to the side.

"What is it?"

"I thought I might bunk here. Stay with you and the kiddos. You've been with them for a few days all by yourself. And, honestly, I missed all of you."

Natasha wraps her arms around me again and presses herself to me in a gentle hug.

"You're definitely welcome to stay. In fact, I have something to show you. Come on." She takes my hand and leads me through the living room, catching the kids' attention.

"Are you showing him?" Kelsey asks and bounces to her feet to follow us.

"Sure am," Tash replies as she opens a door and steps inside. "Ta-da!"

It's her third bedroom, all cleaned up, with a queen bed and a dresser.

"What happened to all of your stuff?"

"I cleaned it out." She smooths the navy blue comforter on the bed. "I got rid of some of it, stored the rest, neatly, in the garage. I figured with the kids here and everything, you might want to stay sometimes. And my couch isn't the most comfortable for sleeping."

I narrow my eyes and reach for her hand.

But she pulls away when the kids both walk into the room.

I don't like that. I don't like it *at all.*

Before I can say something, Kelsey slips her little hand into mine and smiles sweetly. "Do you like it?"

"It's great."

"We helped," Kevin announces. "We each earned a dollar, too."

"Good job." I give him a fist bump, and then the twins are off again, hurrying out to finish watching their show. I focus all of my attention on Tash and watch as she bites her lower lip.

I want to tease those lips. And every other part of her, now that I think about it.

"I'm not sleeping in here," I inform her.

"You don't like it?"

83

"I like it fine, but why in the hell would I crash in here when I can lie next to you all night?"

Her cheeks flush with pleasure, but she shakes her head. "We have kids here, Sam. They're only five, and their parents just died. They're not ready for us to start acting like a couple."

I want to push. I want to put my foot down and tell her that she's dead wrong.

"Even *we* don't know for sure what's going on here," she continues. "I don't want to confuse them. So, for now, this is your room. That doesn't mean that it's forever."

"It's definitely not forever." I lean in and kiss her forehead. "But if this is how you want to do things, I'll be good."

"Thank you."

"Does this mean I can bring my bag in from outside?"

"You packed a bag?"

"Yeah. I'd like to hang out here, whenever possible."

"I'd like that, too." I frame her face in my hands and lower my lips to hers. Her skin is soft, and the little moan in the back of her throat is enough to make a man sit up and beg.

Before I can take it deeper, she plants her hand on my chest.

"I need to finish dinner."

"Yeah." I kiss her forehead and back away. "Do I have time for a shower?"

"Sure. Help yourself. Dinner should be ready in about fifteen minutes."

She saunters out of the room, and I follow behind, enjoying the way her ass sways back and forth in those jeans.

Thinking about her nonstop while I should be doing my job probably isn't the smartest idea, but I can't get her out of my mind. It's like she's permanently stuck there, front and center, in my brain. Everything reminds me of her. The minute I shift my focus to something else, she pops right back in again.

I'm obsessed.

After only one weekend together.

I walk back into the house with my bag and set it on the bed. I set my few personal things in dresser drawers, my toothbrush in the bathroom next to the Mickey and Minnie Mouse toothbrushes.

Looks like I'm sharing with the kiddos.

"You can use my bathroom." I turn at Tash's voice and find her leaning her shoulder against the doorjamb. "It's a little tidier."

"Okay." I straighten and lean on the counter. "I missed you this week."

"Yeah?" Her smile is bright and happy. "Well, that's nice to hear. I missed you, too. Now, come get some dinner."

"Yes, ma'am."

"I DON'T WANT you to wake Auntie Tash," I say as I lift Kelsey onto the countertop and let her sit there to *help*. "She worked really hard this week. She deserves a day to sleep in."

"Are we gonna make her breakfast?" Kelsey asks with a whisper. Kevin is still in bed, as well.

It seems Kelsey and I are the early risers.

"Yes. We're making some waffles, bacon, and fruit. How does that sound?"

"She likes waffles," Kelsey replies. "They're her favorite."

"How do you know that?"

"Because one time, she took us to the diner as a treat, and she told us that waffles are her favorite for breakfast. She didn't have any that day, though."

"How come?"

"She said she wasn't hungwy, but I think she was sad." Kelsey drops her gaze to the floor. "Sometimes, Auntie Tash is sad when she thinks we don't see."

"Everyone is getting used to new things," I remind her. "What's your favorite breakfast?"

"Waffles," she says.

"Then this is your lucky day. Because waffles are my specialty."

We get to work on breakfast, and I enlist Kelsey's help when it comes to stirring and tasting.

"What're you doing?"

We turn to see Kevin, rubbing his eyes, standing at the end of the island.

"Making breakfast for Auntie Tash. But shhh. We don't want to wake her up."

Kevin's eyes clear from the sleep, and he rubs his hands together. "Can I help?"

"Sure. It's a team effort."

"Is it Auntie Tash's birthday?" Kevin asks.

"No, we're just doing something nice for her because we love her," I tell him.

"She always lets me sleep with her after I've had a bad dream," Kevin says softly. "And she doesn't ever yell at us, even when I've been bad on purpose."

"She gave me the last gwape," Kelsey says. "She was eating them as a snack, and I wanted some, but there was only one left. She gave it to me."

"Did that make you feel special?"

"Yeah." Kelsey smiles. "She always does stuff like that."

"See, this is why we're making her a special breakfast," I inform them, happy that I have this time alone with them. I know that Natasha is a great parent, but it's always good to hear it from the kids. To know that they are being well taken care of and that they feel loved and safe. "How about if we make her a tray and take her breakfast in bed?"

"People do that?" Kelsey asks.

"Sure. On special occasions."

"Okay," she decides and gets to work helping me load a tray to take to Tash.

The kids follow me down the hallway, and I nudge the door open and poke my head inside.

But she isn't in bed.

"She's gone," Kevin says. "She disappeared!"

I set the tray on the bed and glance into the bathroom. Sure enough, she's kneeling in front of the toilet and doesn't look like she's having a good time of it.

"Uh, kids, it looks like Auntie isn't feeling very good. Why don't you go ahead and start eating what's on that tray? I'll be out in a minute."

I close the bathroom door behind me and hurry to the sink to wet a washcloth.

When I get a closer look at her, she's leaning on the toilet, and she's crying.

"Hey, hey." I press the cloth to the back of her neck. "What's going on, honey?"

"Bad dream," she says. She's shaking, and she's cold to the touch. "Really bad."

"Okay, I've got you." I sit on the floor next to her and pull her to me, rocking her side to side. "I'm here, and I've got you."

"They died again," she says and starts to cry once more. "But this time, it was all of them. Even you."

"I'm sorry, baby."

"It made me sick. Almost didn't make it in here."

"Okay. It's okay." I rub circles on her back and hold her close. "Just a horrible dream."

"Yeah." She sighs and wipes her nose. "Do I smell waffles?"

"Yeah, we made you some."

"Who did?"

"The three of us. Well, Kevin slept through a lot of it, but he helped, too. I thought we'd let you sleep in for a bit, but it turns out I should have woken you up."

"That's a sweet thought." She sighs. "The dreams had stopped, you know? I had the nightmares a lot the first few weeks, but they'd stopped. Now, they're happening again, and it sucks. I feel awful because I know the kids have them, too. It's horrible for *me*. I can't even imagine how awful it is for them."

"They're okay," I assure her. "And so are you."

"Yeah. Maybe waffles will help."

"I guarantee it." I kiss her forehead and then lift her to her feet.

"Why are you up so early? You were exhausted last night."

"I slept like a log. I always get up early."

"If you make me waffles on the regular, I suppose I can live with the fact that you're a morning person."

"You're so considerate."

"I know." She takes a deep breath, and leans over and kisses my shoulder. "Thanks for being here."

"You're welcome."

CHAPTER 7

"Should I start a real fire so I can put it out?"

I gape down at Kevin and then squat next to him, making him look me in the eyes.

"No. Absolutely not. You're a *pretend* fireman because it's Halloween. You're not a real one, do you understand me?"

"Yeah." He looks down in disappointment. "But, someday, I want to be a real fireman like Uncle Sam."

"I know you do." I kiss his little head and then turn back to Kelsey, who's been admiring her cowgirl outfit in the mirror. "I think we're almost ready to go to the fire hall."

"Are we gonna go twick or tweating?" Kelsey asks as she hugs her hobbyhorse to her and kisses its cheek.

"Yes, after we go to the fire hall to see Uncle Sam." I fluff her hair one more time, loving the way the spiral curls bounce back into place. "And we had a deal that you each get to eat *one* piece of candy tonight. You have to save the rest for later, right?"

"Can we have one at the hall and one when we get home?" Kevin asks, always the negotiator.

"We'll see. Get your hats on and let's go."

Once in the car, the kids are excited. They talk about the candy they're going to get and how they like their costumes.

I can't help but breathe a sigh of relief. Today has been *stressful*. I wanted Halloween to be special for the kids, the way their mom always made it. This was the first thing that Monica didn't have planned in advance, so we had to come up with costumes and décor and everything.

My best friend was more than organized. The woman had lists for her lists. She planned way ahead. But she knew that the kids would grow and change their minds about what they wanted to be for the holiday.

I had no blueprint to use for this.

And I didn't want to screw it up.

So, I've been worried all day. But their happy giggles and excitement helps to calm me down, just a little.

"There're a lot of people here," I murmur as I search for a parking spot. Every year, the fire department hosts a trunk or treat, a safe place for kids to come and get candy, see the trucks, and spend time with the firemen.

Kevin has been beside himself with excitement. He's all about the firemen life these days, thanks to the many hours Sam spends with him, telling the boy all about his job.

I love listening in. Sam doesn't speak to the kids like they're just silly children. He treats them like *people*.

"Stay with me," I warn them as we all get out of the car. "Take my hands."

They flank me, each taking a hand, and we walk into the hall. It's a cacophony of sound and movement. Little Ninja Turtles and Disney princesses run around, carrying bags and making all the noise in the world.

"You're here," Sam says with an excited grin and holds out his arms for hugs from the twins. "I almost didn't recognize you."

"I'm Kelsey," the little girl says with a giggle. "I'm a cowgirl."

"The prettiest cowgirl I've ever seen." Sam kisses her cheek and then looks around as if he can't see Kevin. "Where's your brother?"

"I'm right here," Kevin says with a laugh.

"Oh, I'm sorry, I just thought you were one of my work buddies." Sam winks at me. "You guys look great. Did Auntie Tash help you get ready?"

"Yeah." Kelsey thrusts her horse in Sam's face. "Kiss Spwinkles."

"Who's Sprinkles?"

"My horse."

"Oh. Right." Sam kisses the horse, then stands and

pulls me against him. "Now I'd like to kiss you."

"This is hardly the place or time." I narrow my eyes at him, but he just grins and plants his lips on my cheek.

"Later, I'm going to do all kinds of things that are completely inappropriate for an audience."

He pulls back and winks at me, then turns back to the kids.

"Who wants to see the firetrucks?"

"Me," the twins say in unison, and I watch as Sam leads them away.

"Here you are." Fallon joins me and smiles as her daughter hurries to catch up with Kevin and Kelsey. "Sorry, we ran into traffic."

I frown at her. "In Cunningham Falls?"

"Got stuck behind a tractor on the highway."

"Ah." I nod knowingly. "Yeah, been there. Is Isha a puppy?"

"Yes, she was insistent that since I won't let her get a puppy, she would *be* a puppy."

I laugh and then watch in concern as Fallon rubs her belly. "Are you okay?"

"Yeah, we're getting so close. I'm just uncomfortable all the time. I think I need a Snickers."

"I'm quite sure we can find a few around here somewhere."

Sure enough, we find a big bowl of candy bars and help ourselves to a few while we wait for Sam to show the kids everything there is to see.

"Are you sure you'll feel good enough to go trick or treating around my neighborhood?" I ask her when she rubs her belly again. "If you want to go home, I'll take Isha with us, and bring her home later."

"No, the walking is good for me," Fallon says.

The kids come running over to show us their loot and talk about everything they got to see.

"Can we go get more candy now?" Kevin asks.

"Who's this little cowgirl?"

I glance over to see Seth King smiling down at Kelsey.

"It's me! Kelsey."

"Well, you look just like you should be riding a *real* horse. Maybe you guys could come out to the ranch, and I'll put the kids on a horse."

"Can we?" Kelsey grabs my arm and pulls. "Please, please, *please* can we?"

"Sure." I smile at Seth gratefully. "We'd like that."

"Cool. Be safe tonight, guys. And don't eat *all* the candy. Save some for the rest of us."

We wave and leave the fire hall. I was hoping to see Sam one more time, but he seems to be off with some other kids.

Just as we reach my car, I hear someone calling my name.

I turn to find Sam running out to meet me. Good God, the way that man fills out his CFFD T-shirt should be illegal.

"Did we forget something?" I ask when he reaches me.

"Hell yes, you did." He kisses me. Not on the cheek. And not lightly.

He cups my face and sinks into me in that way he does when it seems as if he's trying to consume me.

It makes me dizzy. Makes me want much, much more.

"There. That'll hold me over." He smiles down at me, waves at the kids, and runs back into the fire hall.

Fallon beeps her horn, waking me from this fuzzy haze of lust.

"Oh, sorry. Coming."

The drive back to my place doesn't take long. Fallon pulls into the driveway behind me, and we meet up on the sidewalk.

"I planned to just basically go around the block," I say to my friend. "They'll get plenty of candy. And it's a little chilly tonight, anyway."

"Sounds good to me." We fall into step, the kids bouncing ahead of us. We wait on the sidewalk as they make their way to my neighbor's front door to say, "*Trick or treat!*"

"So, how are things going?" Fallon asks.

"Good, actually." I laugh when Kelsey stares down into her bag to see what someone dropped inside. "Things have calmed down a lot since the start of the school year. We're almost in a routine. Kids are doing well in kindergarten, and I'm actually managing to keep it all together at home. Sam stays with us when he's not at work. It's *normal*."

"That's awesome," Fallon says.

"I will admit, though, I'm not looking forward to the holidays." We walk down the sidewalk to the next house. "I was a mess today. Worried about making Halloween just so, just the way Monica would do it. I wanted it to be familiar and special for them. And now I get to feel like this for the next two months. I'm not excited for it at all."

"Hmm, I don't think I agree with this approach," she says. "Who says you have to do everything the way Monica did or would? You're *not* her, Tash. I think you need to make it fun for all of you, get the kids involved, and make new memories. New traditions. If you do the alternative, you'll only make yourself crazy. There's enough to be sad about right now. Let yourself enjoy the holidays."

I take a deep breath and let it out slowly. "Yeah, you're right. I just don't want them to think that I'm trying to erase their parents."

"They're five," she reminds me. "They will enjoy it if *you* do. If you're a basket case, it won't be fun for any of you."

"Thanks." I wrap my arm around her shoulders and give her a squeeze. "I needed that reminder."

"Now, tell me what I *really* want to know." She grins at me. "How are things with Sam? If that kiss was any indication, I'd say you're doing well."

"We're doing well." I shrug and then return her smile with one of my own. "He's pretty great."

"Super into you," she says. "It's sweet to watch."

It's pretty sweet from my side of things, too.

"Ouch."

I frown at Fallon. We just turned the corner to go back to my house, but she's stopped on the sidewalk, holding her belly.

"What's wrong?"

"Well, it would appear that my water just broke."

"Are you *kidding me?*"

"This isn't something to joke about." She blows out a breath. "I guess I'd better get to the hospital. I need to call Noah."

"I'll call Noah." I pull my phone out of my pocket, dial his number, and then walk slowly beside Fallon as she makes her way to her car. "You're *not* driving yourself."

"Well, no. But I have a bag packed in here, just in case. Crap, I need Noah's parents to come get Isha for us. We have a plan in place."

"It's all going to be fine."

"Hello?"

"Hey, Noah, this is Tash. Fallon's in labor. Her water just broke."

"Awesome," he says. "Where is she?"

"We're at my house."

"I'll call my mom to come get Isha and pick her up from your place. Be there in twenty."

"Can you wait twenty minutes?" I ask Fallon.

"Of course," she says. "We're hours away from the grand finale."

SHE ALMOST HAD the baby in my driveway.

The kids are asleep in their room. The house is quiet. And I'm in bed, thinking about everything that happened this evening.

I had to call the ambulance, and Sam was on the team that arrived. When they got her onto the gurney, Fallon was already crowning and ready to push.

Noah arrived just before they drove to the hospital.

Thirty minutes later, Noah's mom, Susan, arrived to get Isha, and told me that Fallon had already given birth to a baby boy.

I still can't believe it.

I turn over onto my side and stare out the window at the full moon.

I should be asleep. If I don't get some rest, tomorrow will *suck*. But I'm wide-awake, and my brain just won't turn off.

My bedroom door silently opens, then is closed again and locked. Moments later, Sam slips into the bed behind me. He hasn't slept in the guest room even once since I spiffed it all up for him.

Instead, he waits for the kids to fall asleep and then comes in here with me.

In the six weeks that this has been our routine, neither of the kids has asked to sleep with me, which seems completely impossible. Then again, maybe they've grown out of the nightmares and are happy in their room.

God, I hope that's the case.

"Why aren't you sleeping?" Sam whispers in my ear.

"Too much action tonight." I wiggle onto my back and cup his cheek. His eyes shine in the moonlight. "Did you deliver the baby?"

"Almost," he admits. "It was close. She delivered about five minutes after we arrived at the hospital."

"That's *crazy*. How is it even possible to have a baby that fast?"

"This was her second. I've seen it happen that fast before on a second pregnancy. You were so calm and collected."

I blink up at him. "I was *not*."

"You seemed like it."

"I was in a panic. What if she had that baby in my driveway?"

"Well, you would have brought her inside, and she would have had the baby in the house. But that's not what happened, so it's okay."

"I'm not qualified for that situation." I smile when Sam's hand drifts down my side to the hem of my nightgown, and he starts to caress my bare skin. "Did you have fun tonight?"

"The kids are always fun," he says and leans down to

nibble on my ear. "And the ambulance ride was exciting. But this, right here, is what I've been looking forward to all night."

"Making out with me in bed?"

"Hmm." His thumb brushes over my hard nipple, and he groans. "For starters."

He pulls my nightshirt up and over my head, and then makes quick work of getting my panties down my legs.

"Do you have any idea how fucking sexy you are?" He licks my collarbone. "You make me crazy. I wanted to fuck you in a firetruck tonight."

"That might be interesting."

"I can't get enough of you. Can't keep my hands off of you." He nibbles my shoulder as his hand travels over my pubis and down into my folds. "You're always ready for me."

"I mean, you turn me on, Sam." I swallow hard as he flips me onto my stomach and starts to kiss down my spine. The first time he did this, I almost came out of my skin. He knows it gets to me in the best way possible.

He just *knows.*

"I'm going to make you crazy," he whispers in my ear. "And the best part is, you can't make any noise. Don't want to wake the kids."

"I had no idea that you were a sadist," I reply, earning a chuckle in response. The sheets are crisp and cool under my hot body.

And Sam's hands are *everywhere.*

They roam over my back, my ass, and all the while, his mouth does the most delicious things to me.

I want him.

Now.

I arch my ass in invitation, but he just bites the globe of my left cheek.

"Patience," he says.

"I'm fresh out," I reply. "Sam, you're killing me here."

"That's the goal." His tongue slides over the skin where my ass meets my thigh, and I sigh. Then he travels inward, and I hold my breath in anticipation.

Because every single time he does this to me, I have the best orgasm of my damn life.

Every. Time.

But he switches it up on me, and instead of using his mouth, he just plays.

With his fingers.

Which is no less amazing, I have to admit.

"Sam."

"Getting there."

Finally, he boosts my butt into the air, and with his hand pressed to the small of my back, he slides right inside of me.

Each time is like the first time.

I gasp.

He sighs.

And we fall into a rhythm of push and pull that just feels *amazing.* After I come for the first time, he pulls out and rolls me over, pins my hands above my head and slides back in, his gaze riveted to mine in the moonlight as he fucks me wild.

We don't make much noise. I don't want to wake the kids. But our breaths are ragged, and when he leans in to press his lips to mine, I know without a doubt that I'm only moments away from falling over the edge all over again.

"Do it," he whispers. "Go over."

I have to press my lips together to keep from crying out as the orgasm flows over me like a tidal wave. When I surface, Sam's there, holding onto me as he follows me over.

"Jesus," he whispers. "It's just never enough. Am I nuts?"

"No." I push his hair off of his forehead. "You're not nuts."

He kisses me softly and then leaves the bed to clean up, unlocking the door just in case someone needs us.

Sam informed me that it's safest to sleep with the door closed in case there is ever a fire. So, that's what we do.

But the kids know they can come in if they ever need me.

I pull my nightgown back over my head and grab a clean pair of panties.

When Sam climbs back into bed, wearing his boxer shorts and a T-shirt, he pulls me to him. I rest my head on his chest, finally feeling sleepy.

"Nothing like a good time with you to make me sleepy."

He chuckles. "I do what I can. Wait, does that mean I'm boring."

"No. Not even a little bit." I kiss his chest. "Life is not boring with you in it."

He kisses my forehead. "What's on tap for tomorrow?"

"Thankfully, Halloween fell on a weekend this year. But the twins have a birthday party to go to in the afternoon. It's at the bouncy house place. I'm praying for no broken bones."

"Nah, they'll be fine. They're young. Seth was at the fire hall tonight. He said he mentioned horse riding to you guys."

"We saw him, too."

"He invited us to come out on Sunday. Does that work?"

"Are you kidding? The bouncy place *and* horses in one weekend? The kids will be thrilled. It'll be fun."

"Okay. Weekend plans are set, then."

We're quiet for a long moment, and then his arms tighten around me.

"You okay?"

"Yeah. Just glad you're here with me." He kisses my head. "I couldn't do this by myself."

"And you don't have to."

CHAPTER 8

~SAM~

"*E*xcuse me."

I crack open one eye and find a little boy with his cheek next to mine, watching me closely. He's still standing on the floor, leaning on my pillow, staring at me with big blue eyes full of tears. I frown and run my finger down his soft cheek.

"Hey, buddy, what's up?"

"I had a bad dream." He sniffles and wipes his nose on my pillowcase. Awesome. "Can I come in here?"

"Sure." I lift the covers and pull Kevin against me, letting him snuggle down. "Was it a scary dream?"

"Yeah." He rubs his hand under his nose. "Did you have a scary dream, too?"

"Why do you ask?"

"Because you're in Auntie Tash's bed, so maybe you had a bad dream."

104

I smile and kiss the top of his head. "I just wanted to be in here. Go back to sleep, buddy."

He yawns and is asleep within seconds. I check the time.

It's only three, so I settle in to sleep with him nestled safely beside me.

"WHY ARE YOU SO MOODY?" I rest my hands on my hips and stare at Tash as she puts mascara on her lashes, even though she definitely doesn't need it. "You've jumped down my throat twice already this morning, and you've only been up for an hour."

"I overslept," she says, hurrying through her makeup routine. "I have to have the kids at the birthday party in two hours. We need to have breakfast, and I forgot to get the kid a present, so I have to run out and do that, too."

"I can handle breakfast," I reply. "But please don't ask me to buy a present because I have no idea."

"I'm tired." She sets the tube down and sighs. "I didn't sleep well. And then Kevin came in, and I totally overthought it for hours."

"You woke up?"

"Of course, I woke up. You had a conversation. I'm a light sleeper."

I reach for her, but she narrows her eyes. I can take a hint. She's not happy.

"You're mad because I let Kevin sleep with us?"

"No." She shakes her head and stomps out of the bathroom, pushes past me, and starts rummaging through her drawers for something to wear.

I would ask her if she's about to have her period, but I value my balls.

"You have to help me out here, babe, because I'm lost. And I don't want you to be mad at me all day long. I can't handle it. Just tell me how to fix it, and I will. Honest."

She sighs and sits on the edge of the bed. "I wasn't ready for one of the kids to come in here and discover that we're sleeping together."

"We weren't having sex," I remind her. "We had clothes on, and we were *sleeping*."

"I know, but now I feel like I have to explain it to them, and I don't know what to say."

I rub my fingers into my eyes. "Okay, we're going to handle this right now. Get dressed and let's go."

"Wait, what are we going to handle?"

"The sleeping situation. I'm a grown-ass man, Tash. If I want to sleep in the same bed as you, I will, kids or no kids. They literally don't care. So, let's go have this conversation, shall we?"

"But." She blinks in surprise, but I don't give her a chance to argue.

"I said get dressed and let's go."

I leave the room and find the kids, already eating

cereal all by themselves, sitting in front of the TV watching a cartoon.

"Hi, guys. When your aunt joins us, I have something to talk to you about."

They don't even pause in eating their Cap'n Crunch.

"Okay," Kevin says, unconcerned.

"There she is." I smile at the woman I love, Jesus, I love her, but she just narrows her eyes at me again. "So, we just wanted to have a quick chat with you about the sleeping arrangements."

"Do we have to sleep somewhere else?" Kelsey asks.

"Not you guys," I reply. "You know how Auntie Tash got the guest room all ready for me?"

They nod.

"Well, I think I'd rather just sleep in Tash's room. With her. It's more comfortable. What do you think of that?"

"If I have a bad dream, can I still come in there?" Kelsey asks.

"Of course." I pat her on the shoulder. "Nothing else will change."

"Our mommy and daddy slept together," Kevin points out. "And that was fine."

Tash sighs, but I just give her a look and nod at Kevin. "Yeah, they did. And it was no big deal, right?"

Kevin shrugs, not interested in this conversation in the least. Kelsey finishes her cereal and grins at Tash.

"Can I have another bowl?" she asks.

"Sure," Tash says. "So, we're done talking about where Sam sleeps?"

"Huh?" Kevin says, already watching his cartoon again. "Yeah."

"Okay." Tash takes Kelsey's bowl and walks into the kitchen.

I hurry behind her.

"See? They don't care."

"Why do I think things are a big deal when they're not at all? You're right, I'm totally an overthinker."

"You're just trying to be a good parent, and a good role model. But you don't have to try so hard to do that, Tash. You're excellent without having to try. Just be yourself. The kids love and respect you. They always have."

I pull her to me and kiss her softly, then wrap my arms around her and pull her in for a long hug.

We're rocking back and forth when we hear, "Yuck."

I glance over to find Kelsey making a face. "Hugs aren't yucky."

"You're getting mushy," she says as if she's fifteen instead of five. "I want my cereal."

"Coming up," Tash says with a laugh. "I got side-tracked."

Kelsey runs back to the TV, and Tash pours the cereal. "I'm sorry I was in a bad mood."

"We all have them." I grab a bottle of protein smoothie out of the fridge and open it for my breakfast. "Let's not stress so much about being together around the kids, okay? We're not doing anything wrong, and I'm sick of hiding."

"Yeah, okay." She carries the bowl out to Kelsey and then comes back to eat her normal breakfast of a banana and yogurt. "I have to run and grab that gift. It shouldn't take too long. Then, if I don't have to stay at the party, I'll drop them off and run some other errands."

"I can take them to the party," I reply. "You run your errands. If I have to stay, I'll stay. No big."

She blinks at me, and then blinks faster as if she's going to cry.

I clearly don't do enough around here if just taking the twins to a party so she can do other things makes her emotional.

"Okay," is all she says.

"Are those good or bad tears?"

"I'm not crying."

But she sniffs and turns her back to me so she can wipe her nose on a napkin. I can handle the bad moods. I can handle just about *anything*. But I can't do tears.

Seeing her cry is my undoing.

"Do you need a hug?" I ask.

She shakes her head.

"A latte?"

She chuckles.

"Good God, just tell me what I have to do to make the tears stop, and I'll make it happen."

"You're just a nice guy," is all she says. When she

turns to me again, the waterworks are finished. "That's all."

"That's the kiss of death." I shake my head sorrowfully. "When a girl breaks out the you're-a-nice-guy line, it's usually followed up with, *'But I can't see you anymore.'*"

"You're a dork." She laughs and reaches over to smack my arm, but I catch her hand in mine and pull her against me. "Thanks for handling the kids this afternoon."

"It's no biggie. It'll be fun."

She smiles, and I'm not sure if it's in pity or if she's patronizing me.

Then she taps me on the cheek.

"Sure. It'll be fun."

"You're not getting out of horseback riding today," I inform Natasha.

"I thought you said the birthday party went just fine," she says with a sweet smile.

Of course, I told her that. *Of course,* I did. Because I refused to admit that it was pure and utter torture.

I was the only parent who stayed. And because of that, the kids wanted me to bounce with them, and I'm quite sure I might have dislocated my knee at one point.

I'm too old for that shit.

But I'll be damned if I admit that to the woman I'm supposed to be impressing. She's younger than me by almost a decade as it is. I don't want her to see me as old.

"All I'm saying is, you get to participate in the fun with the rest of us today."

"Oh, I wouldn't miss it." She leans over and kisses my cheek. "Thanks again for yesterday. I got a ton done, and I know those parties are a lot. Like, a *lot*. I appreciate it."

I just shrug. "No big deal."

She laughs and then shakes her head at Kelsey when the little girl walks into the room.

"Nope. You can't wear a dress to ride the horse, sweetie. You need jeans to protect you from the saddle. And a sweatshirt. The sun is out today, but it's November, so it's chilly."

Kelsey turns around without a word and stomps back to her bedroom. The little girl has been so excited to go ride the horses that Tash could tell her she has to wear a bathing suit in the middle of a snowstorm and Kelsey wouldn't argue.

Within thirty minutes, we're loaded up and ready to head out to the Lazy K Ranch. The drive out of town is nice today, a surprisingly warm day for November.

"Do you see the deer?" Tash asks, pointing out the window, and the kids scramble to see it before we drive past.

Before long, we pull into the long driveway of the

Lazy K, moving past the big house where Zack and Jillian live and on to the house that Josh built more than a decade ago. He and Cara have made their home back here, nestled next to the back pasture.

I park next to Seth's truck. As we get out of Tash's SUV, Seth walks out the front door, smiling at us.

"Who's ready to get on a horse?"

"Me!" Kelsey yells. "Is her name Spwinkles?"

"No." Seth laughs and leads us around the house to the back pasture. "No, this one is named Suzie. She's a gentle mare, and she's perfect for learning."

"I want a fast horse," Kevin says. "A *really* fast one."

"Next time," Seth says with a wink and reaches out to pet Suzie. "Hey, girl."

He shows the kids how to touch and talk to her while Tash and I hang back, watching.

"Are you itching to get on her?" I ask.

"Yeah. It's been a while since I've been in the saddle, and I miss it some. I learned on Suzie, too. Seth taught Monica and me how to ride when we were kids."

"I remember. I also remember Monica came home with a broken tailbone after one of the lessons."

"She fell off," Tash says with a smile. "And she fell *hard.* Poor thing. She was walking funny for quite a while after that."

We watch as Seth puts Kelsey in the saddle.

"Oh!" she exclaims and wraps her arms around the horse's neck in fear. "It's really high."

"You're okay," Seth says. "Loosen your grip so Suzie can breathe. There you go."

He walks Kelsey and the horse around the pasture, patiently talking to the little girl, coaching her and building her confidence.

"He could do this for a living," Tash says. "He's always been good with the animals."

"Hey, I thought that was you."

We both turn in time to see Gage walking up to join us. I glance at Tash, but she just smiles politely at her brother.

"What brings you out here?" she asks him.

"I've been renting one of the old bunkhouses from Josh," he says with a shrug. "Rentals are hard to find in Cunningham Falls."

"No kidding," I agree. "It's pretty much impossible. I might be giving up my apartment soon. If I do, I'll give you a heads-up."

"Appreciate it." He smiles as he watches the kids with the horse. "They're so cute. They got big fast."

"That happens when you've been gone for a long time," Tash says. There's no anger in her voice, it's just matter-of-fact.

"That's true." He nods and then shuffles his feet in the dirt. "I've been meaning to talk to you, Natasha."

"I can give you some privacy," I offer, but Gage shakes his head.

"Nah, this isn't a secret or anything, and something tells me you two tell each other pretty much everything anyway." He smiles. "Do I have to kick your ass or something?"

I size up the other man. He's less than a year younger than Tash. He's taller than me by at least two inches, and thanks to the military, has a strong, muscular build.

It would be a close match.

"Not that I'm aware of."

"Good." He nods. "Anyway, I wanted to let you know that I'm moving back here. Permanently."

Tash frowns. "You're getting out of the Army?"

"Yeah. And I want to live here in Cunningham Falls. Need to, actually. And, listen, I don't want things to be so damn awkward between us. You're my *sister.* I want to know those kids, and I want us to act like family."

"I don't know what that is anymore," she says softly. "Mom and Dad—"

"Are ridiculous," he says with disgust. "I love them, but they're being stupid about this whole thing. And, frankly, I refuse to take sides. I get why you don't want to have a relationship with them. I wouldn't, either. I don't see them much, haven't in a few years. The Army was my family for a long time, and now it's not. I'm here for good. I want to mend things."

She nods, her eyes still on the kids as they laugh at something that Seth just said.

"Are you okay?" she asks.

Gage swallows hard, shuffles his feet again. "I will be."

"Well, I guess you'd better come to dinner one night soon. And, it's your birthday next month. We'll have to do something for that."

He sweeps her up into a hug and holds on tightly. At first, she doesn't hug him in return, but after a few moments, she relents, wraps her arms around his back, and pats him there.

When he releases her, he nods, the stiffness gone from his body. In fact, they both look much more relaxed than they did just a minute ago. "I'd like that."

"I guess so." She laughs and nudges him with her shoulder. "But I still don't bake well, so I'll have to buy your cake."

"I don't eat gluten," he replies, making her laugh again. "Don't worry about it."

"I want cake," I put in. "I'll eat all the gluten."

I should have let them have this conversation in private, but I'm glad I listened. I know enough of the situation to know that Tash's family hurt her in the past. And I'm glad she's going to start mending things with her brother.

I'd give just about anything to have even five minutes with my sister.

"Help!"

I turn in time to see Kevin on the galloping horse. Seth is jogging after him, but Kevin suddenly falls to the ground, and the horse runs off.

"Uh-oh," Tash says as we hurry over to where Kevin is lying in the grass. "Are you okay, kiddo?"

Kevin's eyes are full of tears, but he's trying to look brave.

"I just wanted to go faster," he says. "Seth said if I kicked her a little harder, she'd run."

"Yeah, that's how it works," Tash says. "Weren't ready for it, huh?"

"It was really fast," Kevin says, and Tash and I smile at each other.

He really wasn't going that fast, but I bet it felt that way to him.

"Is anything besides your feelings hurt?" I ask him.

"I don't think so."

"Okay, it's time to get back on," Seth says as he leads Suzie back to us.

"I don't want to," Kevin says, shaking his head. "I'm done for today."

"See, that's the thing," I say as I help Kevin to his feet and brush off his jeans, "when you fall off the horse, you have to get back on right away so you know that even though it scared you, it didn't beat you."

"My butt hurts," Kevin says.

"Yeah," Tash replies. "That happens when you're learning to ride. But your uncle is exactly right. You have to get back on after you fall off."

"Have you ever fallen off a horse?" Kevin asks her.

"Lots of times," she says with a smile. "But getting back on means you're not afraid of it."

"I want to see *you* ride," Kevin says.

The kid is damn smart.

"Okay, I will. But not until you get back on." Tash leans over to pet Suzie on the neck. "Hello, old friend. I'm sorry it's been so long since I was here to see you."

"You ready to get back on?" Seth asks Kevin.

"Okay. I guess."

Seth helps Kevin into the saddle and murmurs to the boy, helping him regain his confidence. Gage and Kelsey are playing in the grass nearby.

"You're pretty amazing," I say as I wrap my arm around Tash's shoulders.

"Yeah. I know."

CHAPTER 9

~NATASHA~

*T*hat might have been the best shower I've ever had. It's been so long since I last rode a horse, I know I'm going to be ridiculously sore tomorrow.

Hell, I'm sore now.

But the hot water on my already weary muscles felt like heaven. Thankfully, the kids went to bed without a fight tonight, and I'm ready to plow through my nightly chores and then relax for a while in the quiet.

I shake out my wet hair and then twirl it into a soppy knot on the top of my head. I'll sleep like this, and when I wake in the morning, I'll have damp curls.

I check in on the kids, and see that the afternoon in the fresh air wiped them out, too. They're sleeping peacefully.

Tomorrow's Monday. That means I still have to

make their lunches, ensure their clothes are clean and ready, and I have to clean the kitchen from dinner.

I'm already exhausted. Adding these nightly chores to my already busy schedule has been taxing. I knew that Monica had a lot on her plate, but now that I know the intimate ins and outs of what it takes to be a mother of two small children, my respect for my best friend has only grown.

If I were on speaking terms with my mother, I would call and apologize to her in case I was ever difficult as a kid.

I sigh as I walk into the kitchen and then stop in my tracks. I can only stare in amazement.

Sam is just zipping up the second lunch box and then sets them both on the edge of the island for the kids to grab in the morning. The kitchen is clean.

Like, spotlessly clean. He even thought to turn on the flameless candle I have sitting on the stovetop, giving the kitchen a warm glow.

In addition, the twins' school clothes are folded neatly on one of the stools.

As Sam reaches for a damp rag and wipes down the countertops again, I realize in my heart of hearts that I'm totally in love with this man. Yes, I've had a crush on him my entire life, but being with him, *living* with him has only shown me what an incredible person Sam is. He's kind and sexy. Supportive.

And I am head over heels in love with him. My heart stutters. My cheeks flush. And I would go take a moment to catch my breath but I can't stop looking at him.

I watch in fascination as he pulls a wine glass down from the cabinet and pours some of my favorite wine.

He turns and smiles at me. "Here. You've earned it."

"Are you trying to butter me up for something?"

He takes my hand and leads me into the living room, where we sit on the couch. He's on one end, and I'm on the other, but my couch isn't that big, so we're not too far from each other.

"What do you mean?"

"You did all of my chores for me."

"I didn't realize they were *your* chores," he says as I watch him over the rim of my wine glass. "They're just things that needed to be done, so I did them."

I could cry. I've been feeling overwhelmed, and having him here to help with these things, without even being asked, is a huge deal.

He did all my work for me, so now all I have to do is relax.

I feel like I won the lottery.

"Thanks." I lean back and rest my head on a pillow. "I appreciate it."

Sam reaches for one of my feet and starts rubbing the arch with his thumb.

"You'll put me to sleep."

"How do you feel after your day in the saddle?" he asks.

"God, I'm tired." I laugh a little. "Riding is hard on the body."

"You looked damn sexy on that horse. I knew that Seth taught you and Monica to ride, but I didn't know you were so good at it."

"There's nothing like being on horseback," I say with a sigh. "Even when it's cold outside. And did you notice that by the time I got on, the clouds decided to settle in? It was damn chilly."

"I noticed."

Of course, he did. There isn't much he doesn't see.

"Well, even when the air is cool, it's awesome. And Suzie is a sweetheart."

"You impressed the kids."

"Yeah." I close my eyes and sigh when his thumb digs in at just the right place. "That was a side benefit. Kevin isn't easy to impress."

"I don't know. He seems impressed by me."

"Of course, he is. You're a firefighter, Sam. He thinks that's the coolest thing ever. On Halloween, he suggested that he should go ahead and *start* a fire so he could put it out, just like you."

He stops rubbing. "Jesus, what did you say?"

"That he's not a real fireman and he absolutely can*not* do that. But I've stopped lighting candles around the house, and I threw out the candle lighter, just in case. Replaced them all with the flameless."

"Good thinking."

"Is Kevin going to end up being one of those kids

that everyone thinks is a big jerk and gets in trouble all the time?" I can't even believe I just said that out loud. "Because we all know kids like that, and I do *not* want him to be that way. He's usually so sweet, but there have been moments these past few months when he's just a *brat*. God, please don't tell anyone I said that."

"Kevin's a good kid," Sam says quietly. "He doesn't have a mean bone in his body, and you said yourself that he's been doing better this school year."

"Yeah, so far so good."

"I think the adjustment has been rough on everyone," he continues and switches to my other foot. "They lost their parents, moved in here. New routine, new people. I think, all things considered, they're doing well."

"You're right. They really are. I just worry about them. At least I have a fireman living here, in case he decides to rub two sticks together."

"No Boy Scouts for that kid," Sam says with a laugh. "And speaking of living here, I think it's time I let the apartment go."

Hope sets up residence in my belly, but before I can ask questions, he keeps talking.

"I only go there to gather more clothes. It's a waste of money, and someone else could be renting it. Gage, for instance. I'll have to go through some of the boxes and will probably need another storage unit, but it's silly to keep it."

"Okay, I—"

"I heard from the Spokane department," he continues, clearly on a roll, and I narrow my eyes at him.
"They said I could take through the holidays to figure
out what I'm doing."

"So, you're still considering that job?"

He sighs and pushes his hand through his hair. "It's
the job I've worked a long time for, you know? I love
Cunningham Falls, and I always will. But there's only
so far up to go here. I would like the change of pace.
But there are a lot of reasons to stay here. I'm glad they
gave me more time because I just want to enjoy the
holidays with you and the kids and then see where
things stand."

Part of me is relieved for the reprieve. That Sam's
not going anywhere right now, and we can forget
about the other job and just pretend that things won't
change.

The other part of me wants to demand that he
decide *immediately.* I want to tell him to choose. Choose
me. Stay here, with me.

But I can't. This job could be his *dream,* and I'll be
damned if I ask anyone to give up their dream for me.
That's too much pressure.

"You'll do what's right for you," is the only thing I
can think to say that doesn't include: *Don't leave me.*

Before I do something silly and beg, I scoot over
toward him and boost myself up to straddle his lap.

"Hey," he says with a naughty grin. The one that
always makes me a little weak in the knees.

"My inner thighs are on fire," I inform him with a laugh. "But I don't care. You look too good sitting here on my couch. So, I'm attacking you."

"You always look good," he replies. "And there's probably something I can do for your inner thighs."

"Really?" I cock a brow. "What would that be?"

"I can rub them," he begins as his fingertips drag lazily up and down the backs of my calves. "Kiss them better."

"That wouldn't suck." I kiss his forehead and brush my fingers through his soft hair. "Have I told you how much I like your muscles?"

"My muscles?" He leans his head back on the cushion and watches me with humor-filled eyes.

"Heck, yes. You've always had a good body, but then you went and got these muscles for days, and I just can't resist them."

"You know, it's a lot of pressure when a woman says she likes your body."

"Why is that?"

"Because now I feel the need to *keep* it. Which means I'll have to spend more time at the gym and cut back on pizza."

"Pizza is too delicious to give up," I say, kissing the side of his neck.

"I said cut back," he clarifies.

Suddenly, he stands with me in his arms and grins again. "Let's go to bed."

"Great idea."

～

"MAYBE I SHOULD BE Spiderman when I grow up," Kevin says as we leave the theater. I decided to take the kids to an afternoon showing of *Spiderman* after school.

"What happened to being a fireman?"

He takes my hand and scrunches his nose, thinking it over.

"Could I be both?"

I laugh and then shrug. "Sure. Who says you can't? A firefighting Spiderman might be just what this community needs."

I ruffle his hair as Kelsey points to Drips. "Can we see Aspen?"

"Of course, we can, if she's here. I think she could be in London right now."

I push the door open and the blissful scent of coffee and baked goods greets me. It's like heaven.

"What are you guys up to?"

To my surprise, Aspen *is* behind the counter and grins when the twins run around to hug her.

"We went to the movies," Kelsey informs her. "And then we came here."

"I'm glad you did." Aspen smiles over at me. "Do you need me to keep them for you?"

"Oh, no, we just wanted to pop in and say hi. I don't *always* need something. Sometimes, I just want to see my friend."

"I'm glad." Aspen busies herself making a couple of

hot chocolates and hands them over to the kids. "That'll be fifty dollars."

Kevin's eyes get big. "I don't have any money."

"Well, I guess they're on the house, then." She grins as the kids hurry over to claim a table and drink their chocolate. "Everything okay?"

"Yeah." I lean on the counter to chat. It's quiet in here today. "Sam's on his third day of being on call, and the kids have been so good at school, I decided it was time for a treat."

"You're doing great with them," she says, surprising me. "Kids are hard. I can't imagine how it is with twins. They're happy and healthy. It's plain to see that you're doing a good job."

"Don't make me cry," I warn her, and then we both glance to the door when it opens, and a woman in a wheelchair rolls inside. "Hi, Tate."

"Hey, Natasha. I need an afternoon pick-me-up."

"I totally get it. I'll move out of the way."

I join the kids as Tate orders a coffee from Aspen. I don't know the other woman very well. Because it's a small town, I know that she's a talented interior decorator here in Cunningham Falls. She decorated Ellie and Liam's house when they built it several years ago.

After she takes her coffee and leaves, I return to my place at the counter to talk to Aspen.

"You know I hate gossip," Aspen begins.

"Just tell me."

"Well, you know how Tate had that stroke last year,

and it was a doozy? How does a woman, not yet thirty, have a stroke? Anyway, she got the news that the likelihood of walking again is pretty small. And *then*, that rat bastard she married just before the stroke left her. Walked right out the door and didn't look back."

"What a prick." I shake my head. "Why do people suck so bad sometimes?"

"Excellent question," she replies. "I like Tate. I don't know her real well, just from when she comes in here, but Ellie *loved* working with her on their mountain house, and I've heard nothing but good things about her. So, what? Something tragic happens, and the dude bails? His balls should be chopped off."

"Agreed." I blow out a breath. "What are you doing in town? I thought you were in London."

"We were, but the whole family is making its way over here for the holidays. Callum and I decided just to come now since not much is going on in London. And you know I prefer to be more hands-on with the café."

"The *whole* family is coming? Even the king and queen?"

"Yes, but they'll only be here the week of Christmas. It's crazy. It's tradition to spend the holiday in Scotland, but since they visited Cunningham Falls right before Callum and I got engaged—which feels like a million years ago—they want to come here every chance they get."

"It's a special place." I turn when I hear things

getting heated at the table where the twins are. "What's up, guys?"

"I finished mine so I asked her if I could have a sip of hers," Kevin explains as if this is a perfectly reasonable request.

"And I said *no*," Kelsey adds.

"No means no, dude," I say with a shrug. "You've had plenty."

Before he can argue, several fire trucks go racing past the café, headed toward the neighborhood not far away.

"I saw uncle Sam!" Kevin says.

"Must be something big." Aspen scowls. "That's a lot of trucks."

"Can we go see?" Kelsey asks.

I expect the sirens to quiet as the trucks get farther away, but they don't.

They're not far away.

"Let's go check it out," Aspen suggests. "I'll lock up and get some fresh air with you. It's almost closing time anyway."

She closes up, and we follow the sirens just two blocks up in the neighborhood, just a couple of blocks from my place.

They've barricaded the road about half a block from the house and trucks and an ambulance surround it. Sam jumps out of one of the fire engines, dressed in his gear, and Kevin gets so excited, I think he might try to run through the barricade toward Sam.

COURAGE

"Hold on there, mister. We stay put."

"Maybe he needs my help."

Aspen smiles, and I squat next to him. "Do you see that fire? The flames are going really high in the air. I know you think you can help, but you're still a little boy. You could be hurt. So, you're going to stay right here with Aspen and me. Do you hear me?"

"Yeah. I'll stay."

We watch as the men hurry about, grabbing hoses and hooking them up to fire hydrants.

"Get this car out of here," Sam yells, pointing to a red car that's parked illegally in front of a hydrant.

I watch in shock as about six men circle the car and lift it. *Lift it*, and move it back about six feet.

"Holy crap," Aspen mutters.

"No kidding."

Everything happens fast. The house is burning at a rate that takes my breath away.

"It's going up fast."

"Old house," Aspen murmurs. "They'll have to work to save the houses on either side."

"It's hot. I can feel it from here."

Suddenly, with a hose over his shoulder and a helmet on his head, Sam marches right for the front door of the house, which is currently an inferno.

"Do *not* go in there." I say it as if he's standing right next to me and can hear me. "Please, don't go in."

My heart clenches. I can't breathe. I definitely can't take my eyes off him as he continues forward.

But he doesn't go inside. He's only standing close to get the water to shoot into the flames.

And then, to my utter shock and horror, something inside the house explodes, sending Sam and several others flying backwards.

"Oh, God."

Kelsey screams. Kevin latches onto my leg.

Now, the houses surrounding the original building are on fire, as well. It's a fucking mess, and Sam is still lying on the ground. Not moving.

"I need to get to him."

"No." Aspen grips my arm. "You can't help him if you get hurt, too. Stay here, Tash."

"No." No one is rushing to his side to see if he's okay. Why isn't anyone helping him? "I have to go."

She grabs onto the kids, and I slip around the barricade and run as fast as my feet will carry me toward where Sam's lying on the ground.

But before I can reach him, I'm flung up off my feet and swung around.

"Let me go!" I scream in terror. "Let go of me!"

CHAPTER 10

~SAM~

*J*esus, what started this motherfucker? My guys and I are like a hive of bees, organized chaos as we hurry about, getting hoses connected, ladders pulled, and all of the other equipment we'll need for this massive fire.

The worst part is, the houses in this neighborhood aren't far apart, and given how fast this fire is spreading, the neighbors could be in danger, as well.

"Make sure those houses are evacuated! Do we know if anyone was inside?" I yell to one of my teammates.

"No one inside. They're at work," he replies. "I have guys knocking on doors as we speak."

"Good."

I'd like to punch the asshole who parked his car in front of the damn hydrant. It's a good thing I have strong men.

I grab a hose, sling it over my shoulder, and go for the front of the house to shoot water into the heart of the fire and hopefully dampen it.

Less than twenty seconds later, there's a sudden explosion, and I'm knocked back, flat on the ground.

Damn it!

I can't breathe. I can feel the heat coming from the house, but I can't move. Knocked the damn air out of me.

And the back of my head hit the concrete hard enough for me to see stars.

"Let go of me!"

Tash? Is that Natasha's voice, or is the head injury just that bad?

I turn my head, cringing at the pain that sings through my brain. Sure enough, there she is, being held back by one of my guys. She's kicking and screaming, reaching out for me.

I roll to my side and manage to sit up but have to swallow the sudden wave of nausea.

"Let her go," I call out, and Tash immediately sprints to me, launching herself into my arms.

"Oh, my God, are you okay? Are you hurt?"

She pats me down and kisses my face, and I have to take her by the shoulders and set her back.

"You can't be here," I say firmly. "Where are the kids?"

"With Aspen." Her eyes roam over me as she pats

me down some more. "Jesus, you *flew*. How many fingers am I holding up?"

I stand and make her stand, too. The fresh wave of nausea makes me want to lean on her, but I don't.

"You can't be here," I say again. "Tash, listen to me."

I move us both away from the heat of the fire.

"You can't leave me," she says. She's hysterical now.

"Tash." I give her shoulders a shake, and she looks up at me. "I can't have you here. Listen to me. This is too dangerous, and I have to do my job."

"You're hurt."

"No, I'm not." The lie falls off my tongue easier than it probably should, but I need to get her the fuck out of here. "I need you to get the kids and go. I'll see you at your house later."

Her face registers hurt, but then she steps away. "Okay. See you."

She turns and hurries back to the crowd she came from, and I get back to work.

"You need an EMT," Jess, one of my coworkers, says. "You hit hard."

"I'm fine. Let's get this under control before we lose more."

It's a fucking brutal few hours, but we move fast and efficiently, and with only minimal damage to the two homes on either side, the fire calms to a smolder.

Some of the guys agree to stay through the night to keep an eye on things and work on any hot spots, making sure that it doesn't get out of control again.

It's after eight in the evening when I glance at the time. It's been a long fucking day.

I need food, a shower, and a bed—in that order.

I walk into Tash's house and the twins immediately greet me, wanting to know everything.

"Is the fire out?"

"Did you get hurt?"

"Did someone die?"

"No one died," I assure them as they both latch onto my legs. "And no one was seriously hurt. I'm going to take a shower, okay?"

I glance up and see Tash leaning on the counter, watching me with guarded eyes.

"Are you hungry?" she asks.

"Starving."

"You take that shower, and I'll make you something."

"You're the best." I lean over and kiss her cheek on my way down the hall to the bathroom.

The shower is hot and soothing. My head aches like a son of a bitch, and I'm tired to the bone. But I'm also starving, so diving into bed for about twelve hours of sleep isn't going to happen yet.

When I return to the living room, the kids are in their pajamas. Both jump up from the couch to greet me again.

"We want to snuggle before bed," Kelsey informs me. "But Auntie Tash says you have to eat. Can you eat on the couch so we can snuggle?"

I glance at Tash, who just shrugs. "Up to you."

"As long as she doesn't care, I suppose it's okay."

I eat the BLT and fries Tash made and chat with the kids on the couch, eating around little heads and arms that want to hold onto me.

"Why are you guys so clingy tonight?"

"They saw you," Tash says before either of the kids can respond. "They were there."

"I'm totally okay," I assure them both right away. "This is what I'm trained to do. I'm glad you waited up for me, but I think you should probably go to bed now."

Natasha herds the kids to their room, and I can hear her talking to them as I polish off the second sandwich.

I stretch my arms above my head and then take my empty plate to the kitchen.

"How are you, really?" she asks when she returns.

"I'm okay. Slight concussion according to the EMT, but no special instructions for that. It mostly just knocked the wind out of me."

She nods and crosses to me.

"I'm gonna go to bed myself," I say and hug her, then kiss her lips. "I'm exhausted."

I walk back to the bedroom and climb into bed. The sheets are cool, and I barely hit the pillow before sleep overtakes me.

THE HOUSE IS SILENT.

I sit up and rub my hands over my face, then check the time.

I slept through the morning. Hell, it's almost noon. I never do that.

I walk out of the bedroom and find Tash sitting at the table, making a list and checking her open laptop.

"I'm sorry I slept so late."

Her head comes up, and she watches me. "You needed to. How do you feel? Headache?"

"Actually, no. I feel pretty good. A little groggy."

She stands and makes me a cup of coffee. "This should help."

"So, I guess the kids are at school, huh?"

"Yup."

She sits back down and doesn't look at me at all as she writes something on her list.

"What's going on, Tash?"

"What do you mean?"

I raise a brow and sip my coffee. "What's up with the cold shoulder?"

She stares at me for a minute and then shakes her head as if in disbelief.

I have a feeling I'm not going to like this.

"You know, you can be a jerk sometimes."

"Oh, for sure." There's no point in denying it. I *can* be a jerk. "But this time, I'm not sure what I was a jerk about."

"I was *scared*," she begins and stands from the table to pace.

It's never a good sign when a woman paces as she chews your ass.

"You got thrown by an explosion, and you were just lying there on the ground. Lifeless. No one was checking to see if you were okay. So, I ran over."

I cross my arms and let her rant.

"And you basically brushed me off like I was an annoying little gnat."

"That's not what I did."

"Yes, it is, Sam. You told me to go to *my* house. That you'd talk to me later. Which you didn't do, by the way. You let the kids snuggle up to you and get all cozy, ate the food I made you, and then you went and slept soundly in my bed while I tossed and turned all night because I was damn mad at you."

She sniffs and shakes her head in frustration.

"I don't even know why I'm crying over you. You're *so* not worth it. Not one single tear."

"I didn't brush you off. You were in the middle of a fire zone, Tash. It was *dangerous.* I was disoriented, and you were there, where you *weren't* supposed to be."

"I get it. I wasn't supposed to be there."

"I had a job to do. I couldn't console you or pat you on the head in that moment. I had to put out a goddamn fire."

"I didn't want you to *pat me on the head!*"

"Then what did you want? Because all I knew was that I was in the middle of one of the worst fires I've seen in town, and you were right there in the middle of it with me."

"I wanted to make sure that you were okay," she insists.

"I told you I was." I hold my hands out at my sides, completely clueless as to why this made her so mad. "And I told you that you couldn't be there because it wasn't safe. I wasn't lying. It was damn dangerous, and I wanted you out of there."

"Yes, you made that perfectly clear."

"Listen up, sweetheart. I refuse to apologize for needing to keep you safe. I'd do it again in a heartbeat."

"You're such a caveman."

"And you're *everything*," I retort with frustration. "You're fucking *everything* that matters, goddamn it. So, yes, I'm a motherfucking caveman because I want to protect you. Fine. I'll wear that label. And the next time I tell you that you can't be somewhere for your own *safety*, you'll damn well follow orders, or I'll move you myself. Is that understood?"

She blinks at me and then shrugs one shoulder. "Don't worry, I won't put myself in that position again."

"Tash, what in the hell?"

"You hurt my feelings," she admits and crosses her arms over her chest. "All damn day, that's all you did. You told me to leave, to go to *my* house. And then later, you let the kids cuddle you, but when I wanted some alone time, you brushed me off and went to bed. Yes," she interrupts before I can speak, "I know you were tired. But damn it, I was scared. And I wanted some time with you, and you turned away."

"Not on purpose." I cross to her, but she doesn't open her arms. So, I just wrap mine around her and hold her against me. "I was so fucking tired, I didn't know what was going on. I certainly wasn't alert enough to see that you were hurt, and I'm sorry for that."

"Well, I—"

"I'm not done," I continue and kiss her forehead. "I'm sorry for all of it, except the part where I told you to leave a fire scene. I should have said I'll see you at *home* later. And, thank you for being so worried that you almost took Martinez's arm off in trying to get to me. I think he has a sprained shoulder."

"I'm not sorry," she says and sniffs against my chest.

"I have an idea." I pick her up easily and head for the bedroom. "We can snuggle right now. The kids are at school, and we're all alone. No one to interrupt us."

She immediately buries her face in my neck and holds on tightly. "Who said I wanted to cuddle with a caveman?"

I laugh and carry her through the bedroom door, then lower her to the bed.

"We don't have to snuggle on the bed," she says but doesn't complain when I lie down with her and pull her against me, her head resting on my chest. "Okay, this is nice."

"Yeah." I sigh and rub my hand up and down her back. "You know what would make it better?"

"Hmm?" She looks up at me and I offer her a wicked grin. "Naked snuggles."

"Who says naked snuggles are better?"

"Uh, literally everyone."

"Right. You're full of it, Sam Waters."

I peel her shirt over her head, unclasp her bra, and turn her onto her back so I can look down at her perfection.

"I'm full of wanting you." I kiss her chest, right between her breasts. "I never stop wanting you. It's like a virus that's spread through me. I'm fully infected by you."

"Somehow, that's not particularly flattering." She laughs and then sighs when I clasp my lips over one hard nipple and give it a firm tug.

"You're sexy as hell, Natasha." I kiss my way over to the other breast and pay it the same attention. I love the little sighs and moans that come from her throat as I make love to her.

As I explore every inch of her.

I know her body better than I know mine at this point. And yet, there's still so much to learn, to explore.

My fingers dive under the waistband of her leggings, and I work the fabric down her hips and over her feet.

And when she's spread before me, naked and open,

I swallow thickly and thank whatever god may be watching for making her this perfect.

This *mine.*

With reverent fingers, I touch her. Lightly. Gently. And just like that, she comes alive. The blush spreads from her face and runs down her chest as she sighs and bites that plump lip, spreading those gorgeous, long legs for me.

"Are you ready for me, baby?"

"Always," she moans. "I'm *always* ready."

My cock pulses with a heartbeat of its own as I slip inside of her. I have to stop to take a deep breath when I'm fully seated.

She fits over me like a fucking glove. And when she circles her hips and tightens just a bit, I feel like I'll lose it, here and now.

"Sam," she breathes as she begins moving with me in the ancient dance of push and pull as we enjoy each other.

"Look at me."

Her eyes open, and she licks her fingers and then presses them against her clit. I can't handle it. I pick up the pace, watching with awe as she pleasures herself. And when her climax builds, when her muscles quiver around me, I lean over and whisper in her ear.

"You're the sexiest woman I've ever seen. And you're *mine.*"

That pushes her over the edge. She cries out and shudders beneath me, pulling me with her.

Later, when we're lying in the quiet, still tangled in each other, I know without a doubt that I'm irrevocably in love with Natasha Mills.

CHAPTER 11

~NATASHA~

"*W*hy do we celebrate Thanksgiving?" Kelsey asks. We're all in the kitchen together, all four of us baking pies for the holiday dinner we've been invited to attend up at Ellie and Liam's home on Whitetail Mountain.

I was grateful when Ellie called. Being around friends to keep my mind off the fact that this is our first holiday season without Monica and Rich is exactly what I think we all need.

"It's a day to count our blessings," Sam says and kisses Kelsey on the head. "And to be grateful for all of the good things in our lives."

"Oh." Kelsey frowns as if giving it a lot of thought. "I'm thankful for Mrs. Delgado. Because she's nice and reads good stories."

"There you go," I say with a grin and slip the last pie, a huckleberry-cherry, in the oven. "I think our work here is done for now. I have these little tables set up for the pies to cool, so be careful, okay?"

No one acknowledges that I've said a word.

"Guys, I need you to be careful around the pies so you don't knock them over. Got it?"

Not even a glance my way.

"Yo!"

Three heads jerk up and stare at me like I'm crazy.

"I'm speaking, and you need to listen. No funny business around the pies so they can cool and not end up on the floor. Okay?"

"Okay," they—even Sam—say in unison.

"Can we have pizza now?" Kevin asks. I told the kids earlier that if they helped with the pies, we could have pizza because my oven would be in use all day, and I wouldn't want to cook dinner.

"I know I'm hungry," I say with a wink and reach for my cell. "Let's order some goodies from Ciao, shall we?"

"You're speaking my love language," Sam says solemnly.

"What, food?"

"Ciao," he replies, making me laugh.

I place the order for two pizzas, extra bread, and some tiramisu to share for dessert.

And when we've consumed every morsel of pizza, every sweet bite of dessert, Sam and I crash on the couch in remorse, our bellies full as we watch Kelsey and Kevin dancing around the living room from the sugar rush.

They make faces, making us laugh. Kevin starts to run circles around the living room, and Sam plays like he's trying to catch the little boy.

Then Kelsey joins in the fun, running to and away from Sam, giggling.

But then, they start running laps through the kitchen and the living room, laughing and tagging each other.

"Okay, guys, that's enough."

But, of course, they don't hear me.

"Hey, Tash says that's enough," Sam says, but they're laughing and in the crazy zone now, where they no longer speak English as a first language.

They only speak silly.

I get up to stop them, and then everything happens in slow motion.

Kevin, laughing, takes off again through the kitchen. Kelsey reaches out to tag him, and he jerks away, knocking himself right into the table set up for the pies.

He stops so abruptly that Kelsey crashes into him, and then, to my absolute horror, all six pies go crashing down to the floor.

The twins don't fall. They just look around, confused.

I cover my mouth with my hands. Sam jumps up off the couch.

And if I'm going to keep myself from lashing out at the kids, I know that I need to leave this room, pronto.

I run for the bedroom and close the door, and then let myself cry.

Damn it!

I *told* them, over and over again, to watch out for the tables. I told them to stop running around.

I'm so sick to death of not being heard. Is this what Monica went through? If she did, she never told me. I know she was tired, and there were days she was just flat-out exhausted.

I tried to help her when I could, but it wasn't much. All I did was pick the kids up from school now and then and take them overnight once in a blue moon.

I should have paid more attention. I should have helped more, but I didn't know.

I don't know if anyone *can* understand completely until they've had children.

And now these two are mine. I love them so much, but they also frustrate the hell out of me, and all I want to do is cry.

"Tash?"

"I'll be out in a minute."

"Are you okay?"

"Of course, I'm not okay." I blow my nose on a tissue as he opens the door and steps inside. "We worked on those all day. It took twice as long as it would have if I'd done it myself because we did it as a family. And now they're ruined, Thanksgiving is *tomorrow*. If I'm going to replace those pies, I have to go to the grocery store. Except this is tiny Cunningham Falls, and literally nothing is open this late. What the hell am I supposed to do?"

"Take a breath." He steps toward me and rubs his hands up and down my arms. "Seriously, breathe."

"They don't listen to me. It's as if I speak at a decibel they can't hear or something."

"We're going to have a talk with them," he says. Sam's face is set in grim lines. "And you're going to take a deep breath. It's going to be okay."

"I don't see how."

"Trust me." He tips my chin up and frowns at what he sees. "God, I hate it when you cry, Natasha. It just about brings me to my knees."

"Don't be charming. I want to be mad for a few minutes longer."

"No, you don't." He kisses my forehead. "Let's go figure this out."

I blow my nose once more, then walk behind him to the kitchen. The kids are quiet now, sitting at the kitchen island as if they're about to be given a death sentence.

"I'm weally sowwy," Kelsey says. "I was an accident."

I can't look at the pile of dough and fruit lying on my kitchen floor. "I know you didn't ruin the pies on purpose, but I have told you both *all day* to watch what you're doing. You just don't listen to me, and I'm very frustrated."

147

"Are you going to make us leave?" Kevin asks.

I stop short and frown at the little boy. "What? Why would I do that?"

"Charlie at school said that we're just foster kids now, and if we're bad, you can make us go away somewhere else."

"Charlie's an idiot," Sam says with disgust.

"Sam."

"Well, anyone who would say that is a damn idiot," he insists.

"No, honey." The fear in Kevin's eyes calms me faster than anything else could. "You guys aren't going anywhere. You're not foster kids, you're *our* kids, and you're stuck with me forever. But I really need you to listen to me. To *hear* me when I speak to you, and to stop ignoring me."

Sam starts to clean up the mess, but I hold my hand up to stop him.

"They need to help with that."

He gives me a look that says, *yeah, that'll go well.*

But I shrug. "They need to learn that when they make a mess, even if it's a mistake, they have to help clean it up."

What started as a family baking day ends as a family clean-up day. By the time we find all the goop on the walls and cabinets and under the kitchen table, we're covered in as much of the pies as was on the floor.

After lots of hugs and reassurance that it's all going to be okay, Sam takes the kids back to bathe them and put them to bed, and I stand in the middle of my now-spotless kitchen and wonder what in the hell to do.

I have enough supplies for *maybe* two pies. I could probably do one cherry and one apple. I can make crust all day, but I don't have the filling here.

It's all in the garbage.

Or in the closed grocery store.

I'm supposed to bring five pies. There will be roughly twelve people there, including the kids.

Two pies aren't enough.

I could bake a cake.

"Who eats cake for Thanksgiving?"

"I would."

I whirl at Sam's voice and cover my chest. "You startled me."

"Sorry, you were deep in thought. I didn't want to interrupt."

I sigh and lean on the counter.

"Talk to me," he says gently.

"I don't know what to do. Nothing's open, so I can't just go buy pie. I can't even buy the ingredients to make more. This is what happens when you live in a tiny town. No grocery stores are open twenty-four-seven."

"What *do* you have?"

"I think I can make one cherry and an apple pie. Huckleberry is out altogether because I used the last of my frozen berries from the summer. That'll teach me to not pick more than I need."

"Yes, obviously, you're a horrible person for not having more frozen berries on hand."

I narrow my eyes at him, and he grins.

"What would you need to make more?"

I run down a list of ingredients that I'm missing.

"That's it?"

"That's a lot when *nothing's open*, Sam."

"You get started on those two pies. I'll be back."

"Where are you going?"

"Just trust me, okay?" He leans in, caging me against the kitchen counter, and kisses me hard, then pulls away and saunters out the front door.

I hear his truck start, see the beam of the headlights as he pulls out of the driveway, and then he's gone.

"I have no idea what he's up to," I mutter and begin pulling out the baking supplies all over again.

I put one earbud in my ear so I can listen to my book on audio while I get to work on the pie crusts.

I'm freaking exhausted, and I'd hoped that I'd be curled up with Sam on the couch by this time, catching up on one of the several shows we've been watching whenever he isn't off saving the world. It's nearly nine in the evening.

At least, I'll be able to sleep in. That's one of the perks of not cooking a big holiday meal.

I've just put the first pie in the oven when Sam walks through the front door, loaded down with two paper bags.

"I pulled some strings," he announces. "You know the new bakery downtown, La Fleur?"

I blink at him as he starts unpacking the bags.

"I haven't been in there yet."

"Really?" He frowns at me. "Oh, you have to. It's awesome. When she first opened, she brought a bunch of stuff to the fire hall for all the guys. Anyway, her name is Beth Dansbury. Nice girl. I called her, and she had some pies and other things that people ordered but didn't pick up today."

"You're kidding me."

"Nope." He grins like the cat who ate the canary, opens a to-go container, and then bites into a lemon bar.

"So, what all are we taking tomorrow? Obviously, not that lemon bar."

"This was just an extra." He takes another bite, then offers me some. I'll never pass up a lemon bar. "I have two more pies, one huckleberry, and one key-lime, some gluten-free cobbler, and a carrot cake. Yes, I know, cake is weird for Thanksgiving, but Beth tells me that it's considered an autumnal cake, so it fits."

"Autumnal." I nod and press my lips together, willing myself not to cry.

"Whoa." He holds his hands up in surrender. "What did I do wrong? I thought I was helping. This way, you don't have to bake as much tonight. You're exhausted. I can see the circles under your eyes. And you looked so defeated earlier, I thought this would be good."

KRISTEN PROBY

"It's *so* good." I wipe a tear off my cheek and laugh when Sam continues looking lost.

Tears make him nervous.

"Seriously, so good. Thank you. I can't believe she let you in this late."

"She was happy to do it."

I narrow my eyes on him. "Hmm. I'm sure she was."

"What does that mean?"

"Sam, she probably did it for you because she has a crush on you."

"Whatever." He scoffs and sets the bags of goodies in the pantry where they're safe. "She was being neighborly."

"She left her house at almost nine in the evening after what was most certainly a busy day at work, out of the goodness of her heart?" I laugh and get to work building the second pie. "Right."

"You're cynical."

He cozies up behind me and buries his nose in my neck.

"You're just oblivious when women think you're hot."

His hands roam from my hips, over my stomach, and then up to cup my breasts.

"*You* think I'm hot."

"How do you know?"

He chuckles and licks the tender skin behind my ear. "Because I know. I'm not oblivious to you, and

152

you're the only one who matters. Who cares if Beth flirts now and then?"

"Wait, she *flirts?*"

"That's not the point. I don't care if she flirts. Or anyone else, for that matter." He drags his nose down my neck and nibbles on the top of my shoulder. "Except maybe Jennifer Aniston. I would care if she flirted."

"In your dreams, fireman."

"Nah. My dreams have been full of a dark-haired beauty with the body of a goddess, who watches me with gorgeous brown eyes."

I turn and grin up at him. "Okay, now you're flirting with *me.*"

"Thank God you finally noticed."

I chuckle and cup his face. "I have to finish this pie. But then, I'm all yours."

"Good." He kisses my lips and nibbles his way to the corner of my mouth. "Because I'd like to make love to you tonight. Lazy,"—he kisses my cheek—"sleepy,"—kisses my nose—"sexy,"—kisses my lips—"love to you."

"Okay." I sigh and allow myself a moment to breathe him in. "That sounds like a plan. After we finish these pies."

"Tell me what to do."

"Sit right there and talk to me."

I point to the other side of the island and watch as he does as I ask. He sits, props his chin on his hand, and watches me work.

"Who taught you to bake like that?"

"Your mama." I mix the apples with the sugar and cinnamon. "Monica and I were always in the kitchen with her. She taught us how to bake, to cook steaks, all the things."

"Wait, you can cook a steak?"

"A very good one, at that."

"You've been holding out on me."

"I'll make steak for dinner later this week." I pop the second pie in the oven and take the first one out, setting it on the burner closest to the wall to cool. "Your parents were always good to me. I learned a lot from them."

"They were good eggs." He nods. "I'm glad you and Gage are starting to mend things."

"He's not coming to Thanksgiving tomorrow," I inform him. "He'd already been invited to Cara and Josh's with Seth, which is fine. But I invited him here for Christmas."

"Good. You should."

I nod and sit on a stool next to him. "I'm glad he's moving back home. I don't know what happened to make him want to get out of the Army early. He hasn't said. But he'll tell me eventually."

"Have you talked to your parents?" Sam asks.

"No, why would I?"

He shakes his head. "I just wondered if you'd heard from them with Gage being here."

"I probably won't. I know you think that's weird."

"Honestly, it makes me sad for all of you," Sam says. "Your parents are alive. You should at least be in touch with them. I know it's a two-way street, and if they don't reach back, that's on them. But, damn, Tash, I'd give just about everything to be able to call my dad or have lunch with my sister."

"I'm having lunch with Gage later this week."

He stares down at me. "You know what I mean."

"Yeah." I sigh, dreading the thought of *that* phone call. "I do. I'll try. If they don't try in return, that's on them."

"Absolutely. How much longer on the pie?"

"Thirty minutes."

"Oh, that gives us plenty of time for part one."

"Part one of what?"

He smiles as he reaches for me. "The fast lane."

CHAPTER 12

"*Y*ou're such a jerk."

I grin at my best friend, Liam, as he scowls at me from across his pool table.

"You're just jealous."

I point to the five ball and the corner pocket, aim the pool cue, and sink the ball, much to Liam's dismay.

"Touchdown," Callum calls out, pointing at the television. "I can't believe how much I like American football."

"We won't tell anyone," Liam says as he watches me studying the table.

The four of us—Liam, Callum, Sebastian, and I—are in what I refer to as Liam's Man Cave. After we gorged ourselves on a delicious dinner made by the culinarily talented Alice, we escaped up here to play pool and watch football.

"Did you hear that?" Liam asks, pointing to the TV. "Will Montgomery is retiring after this season."

"Yeah, I heard." I take a pull off my beer. "He's had some injuries lately, so it didn't surprise me. I wonder who Seattle will get to replace him?"

"They have a rookie who's pretty good," Liam says with a shrug. "It'll be interesting. Are you ever gonna let me shoot, or are you just going to work the table all damn day?"

"You're such a bad loser," I mutter and hit another ball into the pocket.

I rub chalk on the end of the cue and get ready to hit another ball when Sebastian joins us and asks, "How are things with Natasha?"

And just like that, I miss the fucking shot.

I step away from the table as Liam takes over. "Things are good."

"You moved in," Liam reminds me and then looks at the others. "He gave up the apartment, put all his shit in storage, and moved in with Tash and the kids."

"Well, yeah. I was always there anyway. The kids are a handful. It's not fair to leave it all up to her. They're my responsibility, too."

"So, you moved in because of the kids," Callum says with a nod. "Right. Of course."

I narrow my eyes at the prince, but before I can say anything, Sebastian adds, "Moving in with Natasha, who happens to be a lovely woman, had nothing to do with the fact that she is, indeed, a lovely woman."

"You're a married man," I counter. "Why are you checking Tash out?"

Sebastian grins, not at all offended. "I'm married, yes, and quite happily at that. But I'm not blind, mate."

"Yeah, well." I watch as Liam sinks a ball. "She's pretty incredible. Strong. Patient. And she's great about leaving the room if she loses that patience so she doesn't take it out on the kids. Because I have to say, as much as I love those little guys, they are a handful and can be trying."

"We all have children," Callum says with understanding in his eyes. "They're a joy and a challenge."

"No kidding. I had no idea until they became my responsibility, just how challenging it could be. Monica and Rich always made it look so easy, you know?"

Liam stops walking around the table and leans on his cue. All three men are listening now.

"Anyway, we're not here to talk about our feelings."

"I love my children," Sebastian begins, "more than anything in the world. But I couldn't imagine taking on the responsibility of my sibling's kids. It's a burden I hope I never have to take on."

"It's not a burden," I reply softly. "It's an honor, actually. A bittersweet one because my sister should be the one raising her kids, you know? She's going to miss everything, and that's so fucking unfair. It pisses me off. But being with the kids, as much of a challenge as it is at times, isn't a burden. I think Tash would say the same."

"And what about the job in Spokane?" Liam asks me.

Both Sebastian and Callum turn to me in surprise.

"It's there if I want it." I sigh and sip my beer. "I have to give them an answer after the first of the year."

"So, you're moving?" Callum asks. "But I thought you were living with them. As a family."

"I am."

"Will you all move, then?" Sebastian asks.

I frown. "I hadn't planned on that. Honestly, I haven't given it a lot of thought lately."

"Might want to think about it, especially if you have to tell them soon. Maybe talk to Tash about it. She should have a say," Liam says.

"We're not married," I immediately reply and then feel like a jackass when they all raise their eyebrows in surprise. "Okay, you're right. I'm a putz."

"You've had a lot on your plate," Callum says. "I suspect you're still adjusting to all of the changes."

I sigh, but before I can say anything, Kevin comes running into the room.

"I was sent up to the man room because I'm a man," he says, winded from running up the stairs. "Because you guys have to come down for dessert. We can't have pie or *anything* until you guys come down. Ellie said so."

"Then I guess we'd better go down," I reply and ruffle his hair. "What have you guys been doing? Your hair's wet."

"Playing in the snow," he says as we walk down the stairs.

"What snow?" It was bone-dry outside when we drove up here earlier this afternoon.

When we walk toward the kitchen and look out the floor-to-ceiling windows that have a view of the lake down below, I whistle in surprise.

"When did this start?" Callum asks.

"About thirty minutes ago," Aspen answers. "Don't you guys ever look outside? It's dumping, and the wind started up, so I made the kids come inside."

"Our eyes were riveted on the football game," Callum says as he plants a kiss on his wife's cheek.

All of the kids are huddled around the TV, bundled up in blankets, already eating pie and other sweets that we brought with us.

"I think everyone should stay the night," Ellie announces with concern. "We have plenty of room for all of you, and the road down to town will be treacherous."

"I think that's a good idea," Sebastian agrees as we watch the snowfall turn to a blizzard. "It's safer to stay put."

"I can't," I reply and turn to Tash. "I'm on call starting at five in the morning. I have to be home, just in case."

"We'll be fine," Tash says, waving it off. "We're Montana kids, and we brought Sam's big, beefy truck. It'll be okay."

"But I want pie before we go," I say and turn back in time to see Aspen and Tash share a look. "What was that about?"

"What?" Tash asks, feigning innocence.

"That look."

"There wasn't a look," Aspen says, scoffing. "What kind of pie do you want? Alice is serving it up."

"I want cherry," I reply but make a mental note to ask Natasha what that was all about when we get home.

"Aww, you want the one I made," Tash says and leans over to kiss my cheek. "How sweet."

"Of course, I do. You worked damn hard on this pie."

"We heard what happened," Nina, Sebastian's wife, says with a grimace. "What a mess."

"It looked a bit like roadkill, to be honest." I take a bite of the cherry and sigh in happiness. "You did great, babe."

"Yeah?" Tash's face lights up. "Thanks. I'm going to have to go on a three-day fast after today. Alice's cooking is always *so good*, and now I'm completely stuffed."

"There are plenty of leftovers for you to take some away," Alice offers, but Natasha is already shaking her head.

"That's not necessary."

"Well, in that case, I'll make a big batch of turkey

pot pie with extra biscuits on Saturday, and everyone is welcome to come help us eat it."

"That, we can do," I reply with a wink. "I'll never turn down your cooking, Alice. Why don't you dump that loser of a husband of yours and run off to marry me?"

"That's a charming offer," Alice says with a laugh, "but I'm rather attached to the man."

"What a relief, as I've grown used to having you around, as well," David says as he walks in from outside and kisses his wife's cheek. "This storm is a bugger."

"We should get down the mountain," Tash says to me, and David looks up with a scowl.

"You're leaving? In this?"

"I have to work early in the morning," I say as Tash gathers the kids. "I'll be okay. I'll take it easy."

When we have the kids bundled up, we say our goodbyes and pile into the truck.

"It's *really* coming down," Tash says as she buckles her seatbelt. "I know I sounded confident back there, but this is as bad as I've seen it in a long time, Sam."

"I know." I start the truck and make my way down the driveway, which is heated and, therefore, clear. But it's a different story altogether when I make it to the road that leads down to town. "Okay, listen up, everyone. This road is icy, and it's windy. We're going to have some shelter from the wind in the trees here, but it's going to be rocky, so please stay quiet and no roughhousing with each other on this trip, okay?"

I look around, and everyone nods with wide eyes.

This is going to suck ass.

I can't see the pavement through the snow covering it, and the plows haven't been out to clear it away yet. But I know this road like the back of my hand, so I set off down the mountain.

"It's pure ice under the snow," I mutter in amazement. "It froze fast. I didn't see this storm in the forecast."

"It was supposed to hit north of us," Tash says.

I gear the truck way down so I have no choice but to inch along. As we round a corner, I see a car off the road with its hazards on.

"They hit a tree," Tash says.

"That's the only thing that kept them from going down the side of the mountain," I reply grimly and ease the truck to a stop on the other side of the road so I'm sure it won't follow the car and slide down the embankment. "I'm going to make sure no one is in that car."

"Be careful," Tash says before I climb out of the truck and fight my way against the fierce wind and snowfall to the driver's side of the car.

I knock on the window. When the driver rolls it down, I'm shocked to see Beth, the bakery owner, looking up at me with terrified eyes.

"Oh, Sam." She swallows hard. "Thank God. My phone is dead, and I can't get the car out of this ditch."

"It's not a ditch. It's the side of the fucking mountain, Beth. Are you hurt?"

"No, just scared."

"Okay, roll this up and grab your bag. You can ride down with us. We'll call a tow for the car, but it'll probably be stuck here until after the storm blows through."

She nods and does as I say, and then we're both fighting against the wind back to my truck.

"We're going to squeeze in," I say to Tash when she rolls down her window.

Natasha immediately turns to the kids in the back and tells them to lift their legs so Beth can squeeze between them to the middle seat in the back.

Once she's in, I shut the door and hurry around to the driver's side.

"Thanks so much," Beth says. "That was maybe the scariest thing that's ever happened to me. I appreciate the ride home. Oh, you must be Tasha. I'm Beth. Sam talked about you nonstop last night when he came to the shop to get the extras I had there."

She's a ball of nervous energy, talking like crazy, but I block out the chatter and focus on getting us all down the damn mountain in one piece.

When I reach the bottom where this road meets the one that leads into town, I breathe a big sigh of relief. The snow is just as intense down here, but it's not as cold, so I shouldn't have to fight the ice on the roads.

"What's your address, Beth?"

"Oh, I'm in the apartments just up the road here. Just before you get to the first stoplight."

I nod. I know the apartments very well.

I just moved out of them.

"I *love* the building," Beth continues. "And I have the cutest neighbor. I don't know his name, but he just moved in. He looks like he might be in the military. He doesn't say much, but he seems really nice."

Tash and I share an amused glance.

"I wish I knew who his friend is," Beth continues. "The one who helped him move in. Holy sexy, Batman. I mean, they're both something to write home about. It's a pity that he didn't move in during the summer when he could have washed his car with his shirt off. And his friend could have helped."

Natasha laughs out loud now and glances back at Beth. "Actually, the guy who lives there now is my brother, Gage. And you're right, he just got out of the Army and moved back to town. He's definitely nice, and if you need anything, he'll help you out.

"His best friend is Seth King. If you want, I can introduce you to him. He's single."

"No." I look into the rearview and see Beth shaking her head adamantly. "No, definitely not."

"Seth's awesome," Tash points out.

"Trust me. Hot guys and I don't mix well. Been there, done that, have the baggage to prove it. But he sure is nice to look at. That's me, on the end." She points to the end of the building. "Thanks again for the ride."

"Do you want me to call the tow for you, or do you

have it?"

"Oh, I can do it." She eases her way out of the truck and then smiles when I roll my window down. "It was nice to meet you, Natasha. Come into the bakery anytime. My treat."

"Thank you," Tash says. "Happy Thanksgiving."

"You, too. Bye." She waves, and I wait while she climbs the steps to her apartment. When she lets herself inside, I put the truck in gear to head home.

"Okay, so she probably wasn't flirting with you," Tash admits.

"She's nice," I reply.

"Yeah, I like her. She's super small and cute. Dimples in those cheeks for days. I wish she'd let me introduce her to Seth, but I'll mind my business."

"You?" I act like I'm shocked. "Mind your own business? Who are you and what have you done with Natasha Mills?"

She smacks my arm but also laughs. "Whatever. I'm not that bad."

"Are we gonna crash?" Kevin asks from the back seat. "Or can we talk now?"

"You were so quiet, I almost forgot you were here," I admit.

"Of course, they listen to *you*," Tash whispers and sighs. "Thanks for being quiet, guys."

I take her hand in mine and kiss her knuckles. "Hey, *I* listen to you."

"Yeah, most of the time."

CHAPTER 13

~NATASHA~

"They're finally asleep. The excitement from the storm and all of today's festivities at Ellie and Liam's house had them all hopped up. But now, they're down for the count." I stop in the kitchen and pour myself a glass of red wine, then walk into the living room armed with my laptop, the ads for Black Friday from the Sunday newspaper, and a notebook.

It's time to make some Christmas decisions when it comes to the kids.

"Have I mentioned that I love black Friday?" I ask as I curl up on the couch, set my wine on the floor next to me, and open the computer. "Because I do. Monica and I went shopping every year. Some years, she made me get up at like three o'clock in the morning because there were sales she didn't want to miss."

I stop and stare at the computer screen, but I don't really see it.

One thing I've learned over the past six months is that grief is a sneaky bastard and will surprise you in the oddest moments. Take your breath away.

Bring you to your knees.

Like after a fun holiday with friends, curled up on the couch as it snows and storms outside.

And a sexy man watching me from just a few feet away with complete understanding in his blue eyes.

"I miss her, too," he says softly and rubs the top of my foot in support. "Okay, let's do this. What should we get the kids? I'm not buying anyone a car."

This makes me chuckle like he knew it would. "Not until they're sixteen."

"Or twenty-six," he mutters. "Do you know how many dead teenagers I've scraped off the pavement over the years?"

"Jesus, Sam." I shake my head and reach out for his hand. "Why do you do this job? It's so damn sad."

"Because someone has to. Someone has to help."

"And you're the helper." I squeeze his hand.

"Yeah, I guess so. Okay, let's do this."

I nod and inhale as I reach for the first ad. "I did some research on what five-year-olds are playing with these days. I mean, I also pay attention when the kids announce that they want something, but this is my first Christmas as a parent, and I want them to be excited, you know?"

"I'm grateful you did because I'm totally clueless," he

says with a grin and reaches for another ad. "Let's get Kevin a PlayStation."

I blink over at him. "He's *five.*"

"So?" He raises a brow.

"*So,* he's too young for a gaming console. I don't like them spending too much time staring at a screen."

"They watch TV all the damn time," he counters, clearly frustrated.

"No, they don't. They're allowed one hour a day on school days, and no more than three hours over the weekend. Oh, Target has some cool-looking art sets on sale. Kelsey loves this kind of stuff, and it's princess-themed so that'll go over well."

"Good one," he says with a nod, but he still looks irritated. "They have some cool-looking building blocks at this store. Complete with little race cars. Kev would love that."

"It's going on the list. You know, we could just go ahead and order most of this tonight. The sales start at midnight, and that's only thirty minutes away. I'll start putting stuff in the carts."

My fingers fly over the keyboard as I look for the items we've already discussed, and I put them in my shopping carts.

"What about this cool dollhouse for Kelsey?" Sam asks and shows me the page in the ad. "She loves the one at Ellie's place."

"Of course, the one up there is a replica of the castle

in London," I reply with a laugh. "Complete with hard-wood floors and tapestries for the walls."

"This one is pink," he replies, keeping a straight face.

"That'll work. Going in the cart."

We spend the next twenty minutes or so choosing several things for each of the twins.

"When I'm out tomorrow, I'll look for some new clothes," I inform him. "They're growing so fast. A few things will get wrapped, but most of it is just going right in their closet. The sales are too good to pass up."

"Wait, you're going *out* tomorrow?" he asks with a scowl.

"Of course. It's black Friday."

"It's a freaking blizzard outside."

I frown. "They'll have the roads clear by morning. I've been driving on snow since the first day I got behind the wheel, you know."

"Are you going alone?"

"No. Aspen, Ellie, and Nina would be recognized, and it's not a good idea where security is concerned. But Fallon called me the other day and asked if I'd like to go with her. I'm meeting her at her place in the morning. The twins can hang out with Noah and the kids for the day."

"If this storm gets worse, just promise me you'll reconsider."

"Sam, it's fine."

"I won't have you out driving in this mess, Tash. It's

damn dangerous, and there are too many people on the roads who *don't* know what they're doing. I've seen too many horrible accidents, so please don't go if the storm doesn't let up."

"Okay." I hold up my hands in surrender. "If it isn't better by morning, we'll stay home."

"Thanks." He tosses the ads on the floor and rests his head against the couch. "I think that's plenty of things for the kids."

"I do think that shortly after Christmas, I'll take Kelsey to get her ears pierced," I add. "It'll be one of her gifts."

"She's *five*," he says, echoing my words back to me.

"Yeah, so?"

"She's too young for pierced ears."

"Some kids have their ears pierced when they're tiny babies," I say. "She's old enough, and she's been asking about it."

"No," he says, shaking his head. "My dad made Monica wait until she was ten to get hers done, and Kelsey will wait, too."

"You're so strict."

He shrugs. "I never thought I would be, but I guess I am. Just a little."

"Okay, no ear piercing, but you get to be the one to tell her that she has to wait five years to get it done."

"I have no problem with that."

He crosses his arms over his chest and closes his eyes again.

"You're tired."

"A little."

"You can go to bed. I'll just order these things here in a few minutes and be right behind you."

He shakes his head, his eyes still closed. "I like being here with you. I can just chill here until you're done."

I smile. I love hanging out with him like this, too. More evenings than not, we end up here on the couch, on different electronics, doing our own things. But we're *together*. And it's so nice.

I didn't realize I was so *alone* before Sam and the kids came into my life full time. I didn't feel lonely, but I was certainly alone when I look back on that time.

And now, I'm *never* by myself.

I can't even go to the bathroom without one of the kids asking a question or waiting on the other side of the door.

I finish the last of my wine and just as the clock clicks over to midnight, I go through and check out of the retailers, snagging some fun gifts for the kids.

When I'm finished, I close the computer and set it on the floor, then watch Sam. He's asleep. Snoring softly.

He should have gone to bed.

God, I love him. Everything about him. He's handsome and funny. His smile can totally disarm me.

We were thrust into this situation, this *family*. A year ago, I would have thought it would be awkward.

But it's not. It's comforting. *Comfortable.* And surprisingly easy.

Not that raising twins is easy, not at all. But with Sam here, working with me, it's not just doable, it's also fun.

He sniffs and shifts his head, cracking one eye open.

"Are you watching me sleep like a creeper?"

I grin. "Yeah. Kind of."

"Come on, creeper." He yawns and stands, holding his hand out for mine. "Let's go to bed."

"YOU'RE in such good shape for having a baby just a month ago," I inform Fallon as we drive from the bigger city not far away back to her house.

The storm had cleared by this morning, and by the time I drove out to the bird sanctuary to pick my friend up, the plows had been out to do their jobs.

I didn't have to miss Black Friday, after all.

"Yoga," she says simply. "It does wonders for lots of things. You should come to a class."

"I've actually thought about it. After the kids go back to school from Christmas break, I'll do it. Are you feeling well?"

"I'm great. I had some clotting issues after the baby was born, but it's all been resolved."

I frown and glance over at her. "What kind of clotting issues?"

"After I delivered the placenta, my body didn't want to clot, and I bled a bit. Had to have a transfusion. It was kind of a mess."

"You could have *died.*"

She nods. "If it had happened years ago, I likely would have. Thank God for modern medicine. Gave Noah a scare, but it all worked out. And now we have little baby Ezio."

"What does his name mean? It's so different."

"Eagle." I glance over as she grins at me. "It's appropriate for our family."

"I should say so. I love it." I turn down the road that leads to Noah and Fallon's home. "Where are you going to hide all of these bags?"

"In the garage," she says and taps a button on her phone. The garage door opens automatically. "We'll stash the goods in there."

"I'll back up to it."

I maneuver the car around so I can open the hatchback of my SUV, and we can easily transfer Fallon's things to the garage.

When we're finished, I toss the sheet I brought with me over my bags so the kids can't peek in the back and see everything.

We walk into the house, to utter quiet.

"Where are the kids?" Fallon asks Noah quietly.

"They're all zonked out," he says with a grin. "I ran them all ragged this morning. They just passed out about twenty minutes ago."

I bite my lip. "I hate to wake them up, but I really should head home."

"They can stay," Fallon says with a shrug. "It's the holiday weekend. They can go home tomorrow."

I frown. "Are you sure?"

"They're honestly no trouble," Noah says.

"This way, you can go hide your things without them lurking," Fallon adds.

"That's definitely a plus." I nod and then hug my friend. "Thanks. I appreciate it. We'll come grab them tomorrow morning after breakfast."

"No hurry," Fallon says. "Have a good evening."

She waggles her eyebrows, making me laugh.

I drive home and take my time unloading the vehicle. When I have everything in the living room, I close and lock the car, and my phone rings.

"Hey there." I grin and close the front door behind me.

"Hello yourself," Sam says. "Still shopping?"

"No, I just got home. I did some major damage today, but it was a lot of fun."

"Awesome. I'm about to get off work here in a few. Should I pick up dinner on the way home? I was thinking burgers from Ed's."

"That sounds delicious. I'm starving."

"Cool. What do the kids want?"

"The kids aren't here."

There's a pause. "Where are they?"

"They're staying with Fallon and Noah tonight. But I want my usual."

"Okay." I hear a smile in his voice. "I'll pick it up and be there shortly."

"Thanks. See you soon."

I hang up and get to work hiding the gifts. Most of them will fit in my closet, but not all of them.

This house isn't that big. It was perfectly big enough when it was just me, but with three other people living here now, it's a bit cramped.

I'm left with about four shopping bags, and I prop my hands on my hips to think.

Where should I put these?

And then I remember. I have a crawl space under the house. That's the perfect place to store these.

I hurry into the laundry room and lift the trap door that leads to the crawl space, but when I turn the light on below, I scowl.

There's about a foot of water under there.

I don't think this is normal. I don't open the trap door often, but I don't remember seeing water under there before. Could it attract critters?

With the mental image of snakes and other things that I refuse to dwell on, I close the trap door and instead rearrange the linen closet so I can hide the bags on the top shelf, cover them with a towel, and close the doors.

I'll have to send Ty Sullivan, my landlord, an email and let him know about the water under the house.

I'm exhausted. Sam and I went to bed after midnight, and I got up with him at five, so he could go to work. I stayed up and got ready for my fun shopping day.

So I've had little sleep and lots of activity today.

I'd give my right ovary for a nap.

I flop down on the couch, cover my face with my arm, and enjoy the blessed quiet.

Just as I'm dozing off, the door opens, closes, and I feel someone standing over me.

Not to mention, I can smell the onion rings.

I crack an eye and grin up at the tall man next to the couch.

"Are you watching me sleep like a creeper?"

He laughs and squats next to me. "You're not sleeping."

I reach out and cup his cheek, but he takes my hand and kisses the palm. "How was work?"

"We only got called out a few times. No one died on my shift today, so that's a good thing."

"A very good thing." I sit up and kiss his chin. "And you brought me food."

"Oh, *you* wanted food, too?"

I narrow my eyes at him. "Hand over the onion rings, and no one gets hurt. You might be the first casualty of the day."

"So violent." He clucks his tongue and pulls the to-go container out of the bag. "Here you go. I'd like to live to see another day."

"Good idea." I scoot back and set the box on my lap, then open it up. "They even included extra mayo and ketchup."

"They know what you like." He sits next to me and opens his box. "I'm glad you had fun today."

"I only had to elbow *one* guy who got in my way."

He stops chewing and stares at me. "Christ, Tash."

"Kidding." I giggle and take a bite of my burger. I was hungrier than I thought and gobble down my meal in record time.

When I'm finished, I lean back and sigh happily.

"Thanks for grabbing dinner."

"You're welcome." He also leans back and opens his arms. I crawl over and lay right on top of him.

"Wanna nap?"

He kisses the top of my head. "Sure. After."

"After what?"

His hands glide up and down my back, then slip under my shirt and under my pants until he cups the bare skin of my ass.

"After I fuck you brainless."

Well, then.

I swallow, and the next thing I know, he moves us, pinning me beneath him on the couch as his hand dives into my pants again, only from the front this time.

Those talented fingers get right to work, fiddling with my clit before moving lower to my most intimate place, gliding over my lips only to dip inside and repeat.

I gasp.

Grab onto Sam's shoulder.

"Fuck me, you're good with your hands." I turn my head and bite his free arm that's braced against the back of the couch.

"You're so damn wet, babe. I have to taste you."

He hurries to strip my pants down my legs. Suddenly, he's kneeling on the floor next to the couch and turns me on the cushion, props my legs over his shoulders, and feasts.

Freaking *feasts.*

There's no other word for it. I thrash about, going out of my mind as his mouth teases my pussy, sending me over the edge of sanity.

I'm still quaking when he's suddenly inside me, moving in and out in a quick rhythm as if he can't hold himself in check for another moment.

He leans over to brace himself on the back of the couch and stares down at me with intense blue eyes.

"You're so fucking sexy," he growls, and picks up the pace. "I can't stop wanting you. I don't *want* to stop wanting you."

I can only shake my head and hold on as he does, indeed, fuck me blind.

He growls with the force of his release. When I can see again, I can't help but laugh.

"What?" he asks, panting.

"We're half on and half off the couch. Your pants are around your knees. I'm half-dressed. And we look like we just made it through some kind of crazy, perverted war."

He grins. "Well, I was thinking of taking you to the bedroom to get you the rest of the way naked."

"I was thinking of getting the rest of the way *dressed.*"

Sam scowls. "I'm not finished. Not even *close.* Not to mention, I'm no quitter. I will get you all the way naked before the day's out, mark my words."

"We have to stop watching so much *Game of Thrones.*"

"What? Why?"

"Because now you're saying things like '*mark my words.'*"

He grins. "Come on Khaleesi. Let's go to bed."

He picks me up, clothes and all, and carries me back to the bedroom.

"I'm a mess." I bury my face in his neck. "I should probably take a shower."

"Good idea. We'll shower, and then we'll work on getting each other messy again."

"What about the nap you promised me?"

"I'm a man of my word." His face is solemn. "I shall make good on the promise, Your Grace."

"You're goofy." I kiss his cheek. "I kind of like it."

CHAPTER 14

"*H*ey, Sam."

I smile at the tall blonde behind the glass counter and nod at her husband as he walks out of the back at Cunningham Falls Goldsmiths. There are only a few weeks left until Christmas, and I need to get something special for Natasha.

Something besides the fuzzy slippers and coffee mug that says, *I'm a f*cking delight in the morning* that I already got her.

"Hey, Kate. Aric. How's it going?"

"Busy time of year," Kate says with a grin. "So, no complaints from us."

"I'm looking forward to January when we can take a little time off," Aric adds with a wink. "How can we help you today, Sam?"

"I need a present for Tash." I glance into the glass

case and immediately feel overwhelmed. "And I have no idea what that might be."

"That's what we're here for," Kate says with a wink. "Are you thinking engagement ring?"

I blink at her, feel my cheeks flush, and then shake my head. "Uh, no. No, thanks. You have other things here, right?"

"Yes, don't panic," Aric says with a laugh. "Your expression is priceless."

"I thought you were going to pass out," Kate says, also giggling. "Okay, let's look at some things."

We talk budget and colors. But everything they show me leaves me feeling...*meh.*

"I know I'm being difficult, and I'm sorry, but I feel like it has to be something extra-special. She's been through more than her fair share this year, and I want to give her something really great."

"We can design something," Aric offers.

"Do we have time for that?" My interest is piqued, but we only have a few weeks.

"I can fit it in. Who needs to sleep, right?" He reaches for a drawing pad and pencil

"You know, I always thought Tash would be gorgeous in emeralds," Kate suggests. "With her dark coloring and gorgeous skin, they would just be awesome on her."

"I like that idea," I say with a nod. "Maybe a necklace?"

"An emerald pendant, but on a longer chain," Aric

says, clearly in the zone. He sketches quickly, his pencil moving in fast, short strokes. "Light yellow gold. Almost champagne in color."

"Agreed, you don't want to take away from the stones," Kate says, watching over Aric's shoulder.

The other man sets the sketch on the countertop and I blink in surprise.

"Have you ever thought of ditching the goldsmith thing and being an artist?" I ask as I stare down at the gorgeous drawing. "This is amazing. Can I afford it?"

Kate smiles kindly. "Absolutely. He wouldn't show you if you couldn't."

"Then I'm in."

"Give me two weeks. I'll call you when it's done." Aric shakes my hand. "I guarantee you'll have it by Christmas Eve."

"Perfect. Thank you for squeezing it in. Next time, I'll remember to pop by earlier. I'm still learning."

"The learning never ends," Aric replies and waves as I turn to leave.

Now that *that's* done, I need to grab the kids each a couple of extra things, and then I'm done. Tash took care of just about everything, and I owe her for that, too.

She's fucking amazing.

She and the kids are baking cookies and getting ready to decorate the house tonight. I'm in charge of bringing home all the makings for tacos.

And, just because I know she likes it, I'm going to bring home something sweet, too.

I walk down to La Fleur and push through the door.

Beth glances up with a smile. "Sam! Hey there. What are you up to today?"

"Just running some errands. I thought I'd pick up some dessert for later, if you have anything left."

"I have a chocolate cream pie, huckleberry cobbler, and some lemon huckleberry bread that is to die for. But no pressure."

"I'll take the bread for French toast tomorrow, and the chocolate cream pie for tonight."

"Oh, that's a really good idea," she says with a smile. "You could make a huckleberry compote to go on it."

"Right. I could. If I was Emeril." I laugh and open my wallet. "What do I owe you?"

"Nothing at all. This is payment for rescuing me off that mountain on Thanksgiving."

"What were you doing up there, anyway?"

"My parents came to town, and I met them up there for dinner." She shrugs. "It was kind of awful, and I was in a bad mood and not paying close enough attention to the road. Lesson learned."

"I'm sorry it was a bad trip for them."

"Oh, they had a great time." She bags up the goodies. "I just didn't see much of them, which is pretty typical. Anyway, have a good evening. Enjoy these."

"I can guarantee that we will." I nod and leave the

bakery, feeling damn good about my progress this afternoon.

I have to stop at the store but then it's home for food, cookies, and Christmas decorations.

I would have scoffed at the idea once upon a time. Monica always used to invite me to come over for evenings exactly like this.

And I always came up with a reason not to go.

I should have gone.

If I had it to do over again, I would.

But I can't do it again. And it's a waste of time to regret the past.

I've just pulled into the parking lot of the grocery store when my phone rings.

"Waters."

"Hey, Sam, this is Bruce Meyer in Spokane."

The fire chief. I cut the engine and narrow my eyes. "Hi, Bruce, what can I do for you?"

"Well, I know that I told you to get back to me after the first of the year, but I'm going over the budget for next year and working on some scheduling. The thing is, I need to know in the next few days if we can expect you here in January."

"I understand." I sigh and drag my hand down my face. "You've been more than fair, Bruce. Can I give you a call in a day or two?"

"That works. I need an answer by Friday, though."

"Copy that. I'll talk to you soon."

I hang up and try to convince myself that the knot

in my stomach is just nerves. The job I've worked my damn ass off for is waiting for me.

I love my team here in Cunningham Falls, and I've grown and learned so much here, but I've hit a wall.

If I want to progress and climb the ladder, I need to go to a bigger community.

And Spokane has a good rep, with an excellent chief, and room for advancement.

It's the right thing to do for my career.

"Then why do I feel like I'm going to toss my cookies?" I mutter and scratch my head in frustration.

Nerves. That's all it is.

"It's time to decorate the tree!" Kelsey dances in the middle of the living room in excitement. "The lights are pretty."

"I want to put the star on the top," Kevin announces.

"No, *I* want to," Kelsey demands.

"Well, neither of you is tall enough, so I'll take care of that part," I interrupt, shutting down an argument before it breaks out.

"Okay, we're going to have a system here," Tash says. "We're not going to just be all willy-nilly about this."

"Willy-nilly," Kelsey says with a smirk. "That's funny."

"Some of the ornaments are fragile, so we have to

be careful," Tash continues as she opens a box. We have all of the Christmas décor from Monica's house here. Tash already went through most of it, but I know this won't be an easy evening for her.

For either of us.

"Aw, look at this." She holds up two ornaments, one pink and one blue. "Your mom bought these for your first Christmas. She was so excited that year. The holidays were her favorite anyway, but she really wanted to make that first one special for you guys."

Tash passes the ornaments to the kids.

"Go ahead and put these on the tree."

We both show the twins how to hang the ornaments from a limb of the fake tree, and then she brings out more.

"This one is Uncle Sam's." She passes me the GI Joe ornament with a grin.

"I've had this one since I was about your age," I tell the kids and then fasten it to a limb.

For the next hour, we pull out the special ornaments, one by one, telling the stories attached to them and then adding each to the tree.

"Where are your special ornaments, Auntie Tash?" Kevin asks.

"Oh, I usually just do generic ones," she says with a smile. "Different pretty colors, that sort of thing."

"You don't have special ones from when you were a little girl?" Kelsey asks.

"Not that I know of," Tash says, and I make a mental

note to pick something up for her. "Now, I got two new ornaments for this year."

She opens a little box and pulls out two clear bulb ornaments hanging from red ribbons.

One says *Mom* and one says *Dad*.

"Why are there white feathers inside?" Kelsey asks.

"Because those are angel wings," Tash replies. "We'll always hang these on our tree, every year, and we'll know that your mom and dad are with us, even if they're gone."

She passes them to the kids so they can hang them, and I can't take my eyes off her.

My God, she's amazing.

Thoughtful.

Loving.

"Do you always know what to do?" I ask her softly as the kids find a spot for the new ornaments on the mostly full tree.

"No." She blows out a breath. "I feel like I *never* know what to do. But I think this was the right thing. Monica always bought special ornaments every year. It seemed fitting to get one for this."

"I couldn't agree more." I kiss the top of her head as the kids turn back to us.

"Are we done now?" Kevin asks.

"Yeah, you guys can watch *The Grinch* while I finish up," Natasha replies and gets the twins settled for the holiday special.

"What do you have left?"

She looks at me and then laughs. "We literally *just* decorated the tree. I have to switch out the dishes in the kitchen for the holiday ones. Put up wreaths and garland. I have pretty snowflakes that I found online to put on the wall in the dining room. Your mom made these cute Santa and Mrs. Claus figurines that I want to put on that shelf, but I need to clear it off first. And that's just the start."

"And you're planning to do it all *tonight?*"

"Most of it," she confirms. "I don't have time the rest of the week, and I want to enjoy it for as long as possible. Because the day after Christmas, all of this is coming down."

"I'll help."

"You don't have to."

"I have some things to talk to you about anyway. We can knock them both out at the same time."

"Okay, that works for me." She fastens the lid on the last ornament box, and I lift them to follow her to the garage. "I thought *I* had a lot of holiday décor. I'm a novice compared to what Monica had. I don't know what I'm going to do with it all. I guess I'll go through everything after the holidays, keep what I love and what is sentimental and donate the rest."

"You don't have to do *anything* right now."

"I know." She points to where she wants the empty totes and then to the ones she needs me to grab. "But I can't keep it all. My house isn't big enough. It's even smaller now."

"Are you thinking about moving?"

She sighs. "Not right away. The kids have had enough upheaval, and I can't really afford much bigger."

"Let me help with the freaking rent, and you can." I cock a brow at her. She hasn't accepted help from me since I moved in, and it pisses me the hell off. "I live here, too, Tash."

"I can afford the rent."

"You aren't working."

"I have a lot in savings." She blows out a breath. "What did you want to talk about?"

More upheaval.

"I got a call today from the fire chief in Spokane."

She pauses slightly in hanging the wreath on the door but then keeps moving.

"Uh-huh?"

"He needs to know sooner than we thought if and when I'm going out that way."

She frowns but doesn't look my way. The knot in my stomach gets tighter than ever.

"And what did you say?"

"That I needed a day or two. I wanted to talk to you."

"Why me?"

I grab her arms and turn her to look at me. "Why do you think? We're—"

"We're what?" Her chin comes up, and she stares at me boldly. "What, Sam?"

"Together," I reply. "You're my girlfriend, I guess. Shit, I hate labels, and I don't know what else to call it. But you're mine, damn it, and if I take that job, it'll change things."

"I won't be yours if you take the job?"

I scowl and want to punch the fuck out of someone just at the mere thought of that.

"No, that's not what I mean. It'll change our day-to-day lives. I'll be here every other week, but that also means I'll be *gone* every other week."

"This job is what you want," she says slowly, seeming to turn it all over in her head. "You've said so for a couple of years."

"Yeah." I prop my hands on my hips. We're still on the front porch in the cold, where the kids can't hear us. "Yeah, I want this job."

"Then I don't know why we're having this discussion," she says, but there's no anger or censure in the words. "This is your dream, Sam, and I'll be damned if I stand in the way of that. I've known you for most of my life, and I know this is important to you."

"You're important to me."

"And I'll be here." She cups my cheek in that way she does that makes my breath catch. "I'm not going anywhere. And neither are the kids. Sam, we can make anything work as long as we have each other. As long as we're *together."*

I yank her to me and kiss her, long and hard, pouring every ounce of the cacophony of emotions bursting through me into the kiss. I don't want to leave her, but I'm so fucking grateful to her for knowing what I need and saying what I needed to *hear*.

For her unyielding understanding.

"Thank you," I murmur as I pull back. I can't help but press my lips to her soft forehead. "I don't know what else to say except thank you."

"You don't have to thank me," she says softly. "This is what family does, Sam."

CHAPTER 15

~NATASHA~

J'm so damn exhausted.

Is Christmas this exhausting for all parents? We've done everything: school plays, the Christmas stroll, parties, gift and cookie exchanges. Hell, I'm going to another cookie exchange tonight, but this one includes wine.

I need all the wine in the land.

I've baked more cookies in the past two weeks than I have in my entire life combined.

If I never see another red or green sprinkle, it will be too soon.

But the kids have loved it. The lights, the treats, seeing their friends more than ever. They've both smiled more since we put the tree up than I've seen since their parents died.

I guess it's been the mood booster we all needed.

But on top of all of the activities, I've also been

wrapping gifts and delivering things to friends and loved ones.

We've received at least half a dozen invitations for Christmas dinner.

And I have to admit, I love that our community has rallied around us at this time, for the first holiday without Monica and Rich, and that they want to support us all.

I'm grateful.

But I'm also so damn tired.

Sam and I decided that we'd spend Christmas at home, just the four of us. He isn't on call at the station, which surprised me because he also had Thanksgiving off.

But that's another thing to be grateful for. Our time together is ticking down, so I'll take every minute with him that I can get.

"Okay, guys, I shouldn't be late." I hustle into the kitchen and make sure I have everything I need in my handbag. "I'll have my cell on me if you need anything."

"We won't need anything," Sam assures me as he sidles up behind me and wraps his arms around my waist, kissing my neck from behind. "Why do you have to look so delicious tonight?"

"I definitely don't," I reply with a laugh. "My makeup didn't cooperate, the jeans I wanted to wear were in the laundry, and I feel like I'm forgetting something."

"Cookies?" He reaches over for the big roaster pan

full of the cookies I'm bringing to share. It's nestled in an empty pan that I'll fill with an assortment of everyone else's cookies.

I'll have to freeze them. We have cookies coming out of our ears.

"I've never been this social before."

"People like you," he says simply.

"They didn't like me last year?" I lean over to kiss his cheek. "Okay, I'd better go."

"Hey." He takes my chin in his fingers and tilts my head up so he can examine my face. "You okay?"

"Sure. Why wouldn't I be?"

"You have dark circles going on. You look beat, babe."

"So tired." I sigh and close my eyes for just a moment, but then I straighten and offer him a brave smile. "But fine. I won't be late, and I'll go to bed early for the first time in over a week."

"You could stay home," he suggests. "Get comfy and lounge."

That sounds like the best idea I've ever heard. But I know I can't do that.

"Ellie will be sad if I don't come. It's her first cookie exchange. Or, biscuit exchange, as she calls it. I can't bail on her."

"You're going up the mountain?" He frowns down at me.

"No, it's at Nina and Sebastian's place." I kiss him

one last time, then hug each of the kids. "Have fun. I'll see you in a bit."

"Drive safe." Sam walks me to the door and kisses me once more, lingering a little longer than needed. "And have fun."

"Yes, sir." I wink at him and trudge through the snow that fell all day to my car.

The engine doesn't want to turn over, but it fires up after a couple of tries.

"Must be the cold," I mutter and briefly wonder if I should have an engine block heater installed. I've never needed one on this car before, but it gets damn cold here, and a dead car is the worst in the winter.

I mentally add it to the long list of to-dos in my head and take off toward Nina's house on the lake. Less than five minutes later, I pull through her security gate and make my way through the front door, cookies in hand.

I love this house. The first time Monica and I came here when Ellie invited us over to help her seduce Liam, we were *stunned* by the beauty of the inside of the home, not to mention the stellar views of the lake.

It's a fantasy, really. And one I get to take part in regularly.

How did a girl like me get to be good friends with the royal family? It's a question I ask myself often.

But I'm not complaining at all.

When I enter the foyer, a server holding a silver tray

full of what looks like hot chocolate martinis approaches.

I'm officially in love.

"Miss," another server says as she takes my cookie tray from me. "I'll just set these with the others. Please, be at home. We have the hot chocolate martinis here, peppermint martinis in the great room, and there is plenty of festive charcuterie to eat, as well."

"Thank you," I murmur as someone slips my coat off my shoulders. The next thing I know, I'm walking into the living room with the best martini I've ever tasted.

"You're here," Ellie says with an excited smile. "And you look *marvelous.*"

"I think you mean underdressed," I reply as I glance around and see that everyone but me is in either a dress or slacks. "You should have told me that I shouldn't wear jeans, El."

"You're gorgeous. There is no specific attire, my friend."

"You mean, everyone but me just *knew* to wear something fancy? How did this escape me?"

"You're in the middle of your first holiday season as a parent," Nina says as she joins us. "I'm shocked that you're conscious and not weeping."

"Oh my God, you guys. Why is it so hard?"

"*So* hard," Nina agrees. "And we have help. I would be lost without Jordan to help with things."

"God, we love Jordan," Ellie agrees.

Jordan is married to Nina's personal security guard, Nick. She came on staff when she married Nick, and as a nurse, took care of all three of the princesses when they were pregnant. She stayed on as medical staff and to help with the babies.

Nina, Ellie, and Aspen all insisted that they didn't want full-time nannies. They wanted to raise their children themselves.

But Jordan has been a huge help over the years and became part of the family.

"Is someone talking about me?" Jordan asks as she joins us.

I love that the royal family befriends their employees—especially those who work closely with them every day.

"We're simply grateful for you," Ellie says with a smile and then waves toward the doorway. "Oh, Cara and Jillian King just arrived. I'll go welcome them."

"She loves to host a party," Nina says.

"Aren't you co-hosting?" I ask and sip my amazing beverage.

"No, I just provided the venue. This is all Ellie's doing. The cocktails, the food, the décor. All her."

"She's been nervous," Jordan confides. "She wanted it to be just so."

"Well, she didn't need to worry," I reply. "It's all gorgeous and delicious."

I know that I told Sam that I'd be home early, but

this party is just too good to leave early. People I've known all my life are here, and the food is amazing.

Monica would have loved this.

"This is the best holiday party I've been to all season," I inform Ellie later when most of the guests have left.

"Really?" She turns hopeful eyes to mine. "I so hope the others enjoyed it."

"Are you kidding? The cocktails alone were special, but then we didn't have to fetch our own cookies. This is the only cookie exchange I've heard of where the cookies were divvied up for us and handed back to each guest when they leave."

I sip the peppermint martini I switched to.

"Will you be able to drive home?" Ellie asks me.

"Oh, absolutely. I've only had three martinis over the course of that many hours. I'm just tired, not drunk."

"Are you sure you won't come up for dinner tomorrow night?"

Tomorrow night is Christmas Eve. "No, thanks. Sam and I decided we want to stay in and start making some new traditions with the kids."

"I think that's wonderful," Ellie says.

"Speaking of Sam and the twins, I should go. But thank you so much for such a fun party, El."

"You're welcome." She hugs me close. "Drive safe. Text me when you get there, okay?"

"You're the youngest, and yet you're such a mother hen." I grin and give her a wink. "I'll check in."

I wave at Nina and make my way to the front door where a staff member hands me a pan full of cookies and my other belongings.

If I wasn't already sober, the brisk, biting winter air would do the trick. It's cold tonight.

I glance up but only see stars.

No snow, just damn cold.

I climb in my car and turn the key. It sputters the way it did earlier, but with some coaxing, it fires up, and I head toward home. About a mile from my house, the car just…quits.

I coast to the side of the road and try to start it back up, but it's no use.

It's dead.

I could call Sam, but he's home with the kids. He can't leave them alone to come and get me.

There are others I could call, but it's only a mile away. By the time someone arrived to give me a ride, I'd already be home.

That's just silly.

I bundle up in my coat, root around for my hat and mittens, and make sure I have my purse and the cookies, then lock the car and set off for home.

"Jesus, it's cold," I mutter as I trudge through the snow to the sidewalk. It's icy, so I have to be careful where I step.

Which means, I have to move much slower than normal.

By the time I make it up the steps to my front door, I feel like my fingers and toes might fall off.

"Where the hell have you been?"

I scowl at Sam when he yanks the door open. "Huh?"

"What the hell happened?" he demands and helps me inside. "Jesus Christ, Tash, you're frozen solid."

"Car broke down." My lips don't want to work. I'm stiff. "Only walked a mile, but it's cold."

"Ellie was worried and called me. Said you promised to text her when you got home. That was an *hour* ago. You didn't answer your phone."

"Forgot it in the car."

He takes the cookies from me and then wraps his arms around me. "God, you'll get frostbite. Come on, honey, we have to warm you up."

"Kinda numb."

"Yeah, I'll just bet you are. We have to warm you up slowly so we don't do any damage."

"A hot shower will do it."

"Not yet." He leads me to my bedroom and starts stripping me out of my clothes. When I'm down to my underwear, he guides me under the covers, then throws extra blankets on top of me. "I'm going to make you some hot tea, and then I'm getting into that bed with you."

"I'm not really in the mood for sex."

He doesn't laugh like I expected. He shakes his head in disgust and leaves the room without another word.

Well, I guess walking in the snow pisses Sam off.

Good to know.

My teeth are chattering when he returns, carrying a whole pot of hot water, a mug, and several bags of tea.

"This will steep while we warm you up. Which one do you want?"

"Lavender."

He pours the water over the tea bag, then strips down to his skivvies and joins me under the covers.

His warm body feels hot to me, but I wrap myself around him and soak him up.

"It's really cold out tonight."

"I know." He rubs circles over my back. "What happened to your car?"

"I don't know, it just died. I was glad that I was able to at least coast to the side of the road. I'll call someone in the morning."

"You should have called *me*."

I glance up at him. "You're here with the kids. They can't be left alone. And it was only a mile."

"On a normal day, that's not a big deal. In this cold, it could have been deadly." But he's not angry with me anymore. His lips are pressed to my forehead. "Did you have fun?"

"I'm so glad I went. It was so fancy and pretty. And there were so many people there that I knew and haven't seen in a while. I kept thinking that Monica would have loved it. And, honestly, it didn't make me as sad as it used to. I mean, I'm still sad every day, but I didn't want to hide in a corner and sob. It was just a thought of, '*Oh, Mon would have had a good time tonight.*'"

"It's good that you enjoyed yourself. Just don't walk home again in the winter, okay?"

"Oh, trust me, lesson learned." My teeth finally stopped chattering. "Did you guys have a nice evening?"

"We watched a Christmas movie and then they went to bed. Pretty relaxed, really. I wrapped some presents."

I look up in surprise. "Really?"

"Sure. I mean, they're not as pretty as yours, but they'll pass. You shouldn't have to do it all, Tash. I know you think you have it all under control, and you do, but I can help. You really need to let me help more."

You're leaving.

I don't say it out loud, but it's true. I can't drop my guard and rely on him now because he's about to leave, and then it'll be all up to me anyway.

But I don't say anything. The extra help that he's willing to give me now is just that: extra. I'll take it.

But I won't learn to expect it.

And I can't get used to it.

"Your brain is moving way too fast."

I laugh and then yawn. "Actually, I'm really tired. The combination of martinis and cold weather have knocked me on my ass."

"You drank?"

"Of course, I drank. She had hot chocolate martinis, Sam. No one in their right mind could pass that up. But don't worry, I didn't drink too much, and I spaced them out. I was perfectly sober."

"I know you're not stupid enough to drink and drive."

He kisses my head.

"Do you want tea?"

"No." I yawn again. "I want to sleep."

CHAPTER 16

~ SAM ~

"W hat about carrots?" Kelsey asks as we set a plate of cookies, complete with a glass of milk, on a table by the Christmas tree.

"What about them?" I ask.

"We have to leave something for the reindeer," Kevin jumps in to add. "They'll be so hungry after all of that flying."

"Right." I look over at Tash as she walks into the room. "Do we have any carrots?"

"I don't think so." She frowns. "Why?"

I relay the important information about the eating habits of Santa's reindeer.

"We have apples," Tash announces. "Reindeer like apples. I'll just cut one up."

"That was a close call," Kelsey says to her brother.

God, they're funny. And they're changing so quickly. Kelsey doesn't have any issues with her Rs anymore. They've grown at least three inches in the last six months. And the things they randomly say have Tash and I looking at each other in both amusement and surprise.

"Okay, it's time for bed," Tash announces. "But first, we have to have a serious conversation."

"Okay." Kelsey gives Tash her undivided attention.

"You know in the song, *Santa Claus is Coming to Town*, it says 'He knows when you are sleeping?'" Tash asks. Both kids nod. "Well, it's true. He *does* know when you're sleeping, and if you get out of bed on Christmas Eve, he'll skip our house."

"No way," Kevin says in awe.

"It's true," Tash says. "I don't make the rules."

I grin, standing behind the kids so they can't see me. She totally makes the rules.

"So we have to stay in bed," Kelsey says. "*All* night?"

"That's right," Tash says and kisses her blonde head. "But that'll be easy-peasy because you have your new comfy jammies and your new bedding so you'll be all snug and sleepy."

"Good night," I say, and after one last round of excited hugs and a reminder to stay in bed, Tash takes them back to tuck them in.

I pour us each a glass of wine and am waiting on the couch for her when she returns.

"They're so excited," she says with a grin. "But I'm pretty sure they were both asleep before their heads hit the pillow."

"Good. I don't want to put Santa gifts out until they've been asleep for a bit, just to be sure." I reach over and tug her next to me, wrapping my arm around her shoulders. "You killed it this Christmas, Tash."

"Yeah?" She smiles up at me. "You think so?"

"I know so. I also know all of the extra work is what has you looking like you're ready to pass out at any moment. It's a lot of extra work."

"I had no idea," she admits softly. "All of the parties and programs at the school, and I'm telling you right now, if I never see another Christmas cookie in my life, it'll be too soon."

"You have close to a year to prepare yourself for next year."

She groans and collapses on my chest.

"Let's not think about next year yet," she suggests. "I might not survive *this* year."

"You're doing great," I assure her. "And it's almost over. We're in the home stretch."

"Thank goodness." She sighs and sips her wine. "The tree is nice, though. I like sitting here in the evening with the lights on. I'll miss it when we take it down in a couple of days."

"You could leave it up until New Year's."

"Nope." She shakes her head. "I'm ready for this tiny house to be uncluttered."

"I guess you'll never be one of those ladies that has lots of curio cabinets full of knickknacks."

"No. I don't like clutter. I don't think there's any

need to have a bunch of crap lying around that you have to dust."

"Monica had all kinds of that stuff."

"I know. And it's still packed away in boxes because what do we *do* with it?"

"I don't have a plan," I admit softly. "But we'll figure it out eventually. Maybe we'll have an estate sale or something."

"Someday," she agrees.

"What's your dream home like?" I ask, surprising both of us.

"What do you mean?"

"Well, this house, as nice as it is, is obviously too small. If you could design and build a home, what would you like it to be like?"

"That's a good question," she says softly, staring at the lights on the tree. "I love Nina and Sebastian's lake house, but it's way out of my league financially. As for a realistic house, that I could potentially have? I don't know if you remember, but Willa Hull used to have a farmhouse on a small piece of property just outside of town. She sold it when she and Max got married. Do you remember that?"

"Absolutely. It's a nice place. I don't know who bought it. Maybe someone from out of state, I'm not sure."

"Yeah, I don't know, either. I think it's a beautiful home. I like that it has a nice yard in case I ever wanted to get a dog or something. And the farmhouse style appeals to me. All on one level, with at least four bedrooms and three bathrooms. And a killer kitchen. Oh! In the kitchen, I want a pot filler over the stove."

I grin, enjoying the hell out of her. "Maybe a bigger laundry room?"

"Yes, with a sink. And a hanging rod."

"I can hang a rod for you *here*."

"We're talking about my dream home," she reminds me, and I nod.

"That's right. I think that everything you've described is doable, sweetheart."

She shrugs. "Someday. I was saving my money to be able to build a house eventually, but then everything happened over the summer, and I'm not able to work."

"Wait." I sit forward and turn to face her. "Are you telling me that you've been spending your savings, the money you saved to build, on rent and other expenses because you won't let me help?"

She shrugs a shoulder. "It just is what it is. I refuse to touch the kids' trust. I know that legally it's there to help raise them, and for their expenses, but I want them to have that money later."

I shake my head in frustration. I want to shake *her*. I want to tell her she's being a stubborn ass.

But I don't. Not here and now. I'll make some arrangements to start paying the bulk of the bills. She isn't the only one responsible for the twins, and I'll be damned if she's going to lose her dream because of the three of us.

"Why do you look mad?" she asks.

"Because you're damn frustrating, Natasha Mills." But I reach over and drag my finger down her cheek. "Let's table this conversation for now. I have something for you."

I reach over on the end table and retrieve a small, wrapped box.

"We're exchanging gifts tonight?" she asks.

"There are other things under the tree for you, but this one is special."

"Hold that thought." She jumps up, runs to the laundry room, and returns with a wrapped package of her own. "Okay, you go first."

"Hey, I'm the one who had the idea."

"I know, but I can't stand it." She bounces in her seat. "Open it."

I do as she asks, not bothering to care if I rip the paper to shreds.

"These are nice grilling tools."

"It's not just that. I got you a new grill." She grins and claps her hands. "You were saying that mine sucks, and you love to grill."

"I do." I lean over and kiss her softly. "I can't wait to use it. Thanks, babe."

"You're welcome."

"Okay, your turn." I pass her the wrapped box and watch as she carefully peels off the tape, painstakingly making sure that she doesn't ruin the paper. "You're killing me."

"It helps build anticipation," she says with a laugh. But when she opens the black velvet box, her smile falls. "Oh, Sam."

I lean over to look at the gorgeous necklace. Aric outdid himself on this beauty. The emerald is vividly green, and the gold is shiny.

It'll look fantastic against Tash's skin.

"This is incredible," she whispers.

"I wanted to get you something extra-special," I begin as I take the box from her hands and slip the necklace out of the velvet tray. "You've gone above and beyond this year. I wanted you to have something that shows how much I appreciate you."

"Well, you did a good job of it," she says with a laugh. "I love it. Thank you so much."

Her fingers play with the stone that hangs down between her breasts.

Aric was right, it's the perfect length.

I can't hold myself back from touching her. Damn it, I can't get enough of her. And with the light from the tree casting a warm glow on her gorgeous skin, I need to see more of her.

All of her.

But because I love the way her eyes light up when I do it, I whip my shirt over my head and let it fall to the floor.

As if on cue, those big brown eyes light up as they roam over my torso.

Being with Tash is always a nice boost to my ego.

And the best part is, it's not false. I can see by the way she looks at me, touches me, that she's *attracted* to me.

And it's a heady feeling.

"Do you know how beautiful you are?" I ask as I lean over, cup her jaw in my hand, and rub the tip of my nose against hers. "I've never seen anyone more amazing than you."

"Maybe Jennifer Aniston."

I grin. "No, she's second to you."

My lips tickle hers as my fingers make quick work of the buttons on her shirt.

"If I'm topless, you should be, too."

"It's only fair," she agrees as I drag her bra down her arms. "I think you should take your pants off, too."

"It *is* Christmas." I lean in and press my lips against the wall of her chest, right between her breasts, where the emerald rests. I was right. It's stunning against her skin. "I think you can have pretty much whatever your heart desires."

"You." She reaches for the clasp of my jeans. "I want you, Sam."

Her voice isn't full of humor and teasing now. It's hot and thick with lust, and she doesn't have to ask me twice.

Grabby hands yank and pull at clothing, and when we're naked, I can't help but take a moment just to admire her.

"Gorgeous," I whisper before fastening my lips over a nipple and tugging hard.

"Let me." She pushes on my shoulders, and I sit back on the couch. She straddles me, and before I can say or do anything at all, impales herself on me, sheathing me in that warm, wet heat that makes me crazy with yearning. "Need you."

She moves fast, quicker than I'd like, so I grip her hips in my hands and slow her down until the pace is lazy.

I don't want this to be over too fast.

I cup her cheek and guide her mouth to mine.

"Love you," she murmurs against my lips.

My heart stutters.

"Oh, baby." I kiss her once more. "I love you, too."

And here, in the quiet, with the tree lights glowing around us, I make love to my woman.

My woman.

And speak words of love and forever.

"Sam." It's a sob. "Oh, God, Sam."

"That's it, honey." I slip my hand between us and finger her clit. "Go over, babe."

She comes spectacularly, bites my shoulder to keep from crying out, and when we're a heap of sweaty bodies, heaving in breath, she giggles.

"I didn't realize that this was funny."

"I can't believe the first time I told you I love you was during sex." She shakes her head. "So cliché."

"I've been waiting for you to say it for months."

She stares at me. "Why?"

"Because I wanted to say it, too."

"So, why didn't you just say it?"

"I was waiting for *you* to say it."

She blinks and reaches for her shirt. "If you would have said it, I would have said it back."

"I didn't know that. How embarrassing would it be if I said it and you were like, *'Thanks?'*"

She starts to laugh. "You're such an idiot."

"It's a real concern for guys." I pull my jeans back on.

"And you think it isn't for girls?" She slips her leggings on and then pushes her hand through her hair.

"Okay, I'm an idiot." I pull her into my lap and nuzzle her neck. "Say it again."

"You're an idiot."

I smile against her skin. "Not that part. The other part."

"No. What if you don't say it back?"

I pull back and rub my thumb over the apple of her cheek as I gaze into her gorgeous brown eyes. "I love you, Natasha. More than I ever knew it was possible to love another human being. You make every day better just by being in it."

"I mean, that's a little overboard."

"It's all true."

She tips her forehead against mine. "Guess what?"

"What?"

"I love you, too."

CHAPTER 17

~NATASHA~

"*I*s this for my dollhouse?" Kelsey asks, holding up the tiny furniture we got her.

"No, it's for me to sleep in," Sam says, making her laugh.

"You're too big."

"Well, dang it. I guess it is for your new dollhouse."

"Can I open this one?" Kevin asks, holding a wrapped box. I don't recognize that one. Sam went out and bought the kids a few things without me, which didn't bother me at all.

He's their uncle.

But when Kevin rips the paper, and I see what it is, I see red.

"Video games!" Kevin jumps up and dances a jig.

"You got him a Nintendo?" I ask Sam.

"Sure did." He beams at the little boy with pride. "We'll hook it up later and play some Mario Kart."

Kelsey is completely absorbed in her dollhouse, and Kevin is busy looking at the Nintendo box, so I grab Sam's hand and lead him into the kitchen.

"I thought we talked about this."

"About what?"

I take a deep breath and count to three. "We said no video games for Christmas."

"No, *you* said no PlayStation for Christmas," he reminds me and reaches for a cookie, taking a bite. "That's not a PlayStation."

"It's a video game console."

"Yes."

Oh my God, I'm going to shove that cookie up his nose.

"Sam, I told you that I didn't want him to have that. He's too young."

"It's something he and I can do together."

I lean on the counter and stare at him.

"And it's not a PlayStation," he continues. "This console has way more games that are age-appropriate for him."

"Great. Okay, whatever."

I move to walk away, but he catches my hand.

"Don't be mad."

Don't be mad? You've got to be kidding me!

"You don't get to just decide that you don't care what I think, and do the exact opposite anyway, Sam. Is this going to be the way it is over the next dozen or so years? Because that's crap. We're supposed to make decisions together."

"That's not what this was. *You* decided and expected me to just fall in line, Tash. I didn't agree."

"You didn't tell me that at the time. There was no further discussion. You just did what you wanted to anyway."

His jaw tightens. "I'm a grown man. I don't need to have discussions with you over every little thing."

"And now we're done here because it's Christmas and I don't want to kill you on a sacred holiday."

I walk away and do my best not to cry.

Not tears of sadness. Tears of rage.

What a jerk.

I start throwing loose paper into a garbage sack and come across one last box under the tree.

For me.

I frown and open the package, and then feel tears fill my eyes for a totally different reason.

It's a day at the spa—massage, hair, and nails.

And it's signed by all three of them.

"Damn it," I mutter and then feel Sam walk up behind me. His hands rest on my shoulders. "I wanted to be mad at you."

"You still can be."

"No, I can't. Because you got me a whole day of pampering. I haven't had my hair or nails done since...before."

"I know."

"And I like to do those things. I've missed it. I used

to get it all done at least twice a month. But there hasn't been time, and I look awful."

"Okay, now you're taking it too far." He turns me around and wraps his arms around me in a tight hug. "You always look great."

"I don't feel like it."

"You need to be pampered for a day. And you should really start doing those things for yourself again, Tash. It'll make you feel more like yourself."

"Yeah. It's just hard to go into the salon."

"It isn't going anywhere," he reminds me. "Monica wouldn't want you to avoid it."

"If I died, I'd want her to avoid it." I sniffle, and he laughs.

"No, you wouldn't."

"You're right." I take a deep breath. "Thank you for this. It'll feel good."

"You're welcome. Are you still mad?"

"Yes." I sigh. "Just talk to me next time, okay? So I'm not blindsided?"

"That's fair. I'm sorry that I didn't talk to you."

"Okay."

"I'm hungry," Kevin announces.

"I'll make breakfast," I reply. "How about pancakes and bacon?"

"With huckleberries?"

"Sure. You can help me flip them."

"I wanna flip, too," Kelsey says as the kids run for the kitchen.

"I need to get dressed before we flip pancakes," I say to Sam and head for the bedroom. "Do you mind gathering the last of the trash?"

"Sure thing."

I hurry back to quickly change, and then stop short.

There, on the bed, is a brand new robe and slippers on the floor.

Sam totally spoiled me for Christmas this year. I know I should stay miffed at him, but it's impossible when he's so generous.

And sexy, damn him.

I bury my face in the soft cashmere and breathe deeply before changing into clean leggings and a T-shirt, throwing my hair up in a knot before hurrying back out to the kitchen.

"Okay, pancakes with huckleberries, coming up."

"And bacon," Kevin reminds me. "Don't forget the bacon."

"That's the most important piece," I agree and kiss his head before opening the fridge to gather supplies. "Did you both have a good Christmas morning?"

"Yes," they say in unison.

"I got almost everything on my list," Kelsey says.

"Was something missing?" I ask her.

She shrugs her little shoulder and looks down. "I didn't get to hug Mommy and Daddy today."

And just like that, my heart shatters into a million pieces.

"I know." I pull her to me and kiss her cheek. "I

would love that, too. But they're with us, in our hearts. And that's the most important."

"I'm *really* hungry," Kevin says. "Can we eat?"

"Sure." I set Kelsey down, who's smiling once more, and reach for the eggs. "Let's make breakfast."

"WHEN DOES HE LEAVE?" Aspen slides my coffee over the counter at Drips and wipes her hands on a towel as she watches me with sympathetic eyes.

"Two days." I blow out a breath and will myself not to cry.

There will be plenty of opportunity for that after he's gone.

"And when do *you* leave?" I ask her. "I know the family was just here through the holidays. It's a new year, so I figure you'll be getting ready to head back to London soon."

"Next week." She cringes. "Tash, if you want me to stay for a little while longer while you get used to the new normal—and let me just say that I hate that phrase —I will."

"You have your own kids, a family, and duties that I can't even fathom, Aspen. I'll be fine." I sound way more confident than I feel.

But it's true. I'm going to be just fine.

"What do the kids think?"

I bite my lip and remember Kelsey's big alligator

tears when we told the kids the day after Christmas. "They don't fully understand. Hell, *I* don't fully understand, and I'm an adult, you know? It's not like he's dying. He'll be home every other week, but all they know is that someone else they love and rely on is going away."

"That's so rough," Aspen says. "Why don't you tell Sam that you don't want him to go? That it's best for all of you if he stays?"

I shake my head with a sigh. "Aspen, I'm not going to be the reason that Sam doesn't take his dream job. That's a lot of pressure, and he's worked hard for it. We'll just have to make it work. It'll suck at first, but we'll figure it out."

"You'll find a groove," she agrees. "And maybe you and the kids will end up moving with him at some point."

I frown. "I'd thought of it, honestly. But the kids have already lost so much. I don't think it's fair to ask them to lose their entire community, as well. To pull them away from their friends and the adults they trust and lean on. I don't have any sort of support system in Spokane to help me."

"I get it. It's a tough spot to be in." Aspen wipes down the counter. "Vicki's about to come in for the afternoon. Do you want to grab lunch or something?"

"I would *love* to, but I have to go to the attorney's office before I pick up the kids from school."

"Attorney?"

"Yeah. Sam and I had some new wills drawn up, just in case. We have the kids now, and we share custody. His job is scary."

I shrug, and she nods in understanding. "It's best to have that under control before he leaves."

"I've just been adulting all over the place." I chuckle and take another sip of coffee. "But let's definitely get together before you leave, okay?"

"You got it." She winks and waves as I walk to the door.

Her comment about us joining Sam in Spokane wasn't off the mark. I've thought about it several times, in fact. But we don't know anyone, and Sam's job is about to become even more demanding.

Maybe, down the road, it will be a viable option. But today, it's not. Instead, I'll just have to come to grips with the fact that I'll be without Sam fifty percent of the time.

But I'll have him the other fifty. And time moves so swiftly, that he'll be here before we know it.

With that pep talk under my belt, I walk down the block to the office of Ty Sullivan. Ty doesn't usually do wills and family law, but he made an exception for us.

His assistant waves me through to Ty's office, and I see that Sam's already seated in front of Ty's desk when I walk in.

"Am I late?" I ask.

"No, Sam just got here," Ty says and nods to his assistant, who closes the door behind me. "I think you're both smart to have this all wrapped up before Sam goes to Spokane. It's pretty simple, really, but necessary in the event of the unimaginable."

"We've been through the unimaginable," Sam reminds him. "And because my sister was smart, things were pretty seamless, legally speaking. We want to make sure that we have the same thing in place."

"Good idea." Ty nods and reaches for a folder full of papers. "Let's go over this, and then once you've signed off, we're good to go."

I sit and listen as Ty summarizes what he's drawn up in the papers. That in the event of one of our deaths the other would retain sole custody of the children, and inherit all the money left behind.

In the event we both die, custody goes to Fallon and Noah.

Once he's finished with all the legal jargon, and we've signed off, Sam and I walk hand-in-hand out of the office and take a deep breath on the sidewalk.

"Well, that's depressing," I mutter.

"We won't need it," he assures me. "It's just there, in case."

I nod. "I bet Monica and Rich didn't think they'd need it either."

"No, I'm sure they didn't." Sam kisses my temple. "Lunch?"

"That's the second invitation I've had today." I force a smile but don't feel particularly happy. I want to go home, get into bed, and pull the covers over my head. "Sure. What should we get?"

"Chinese." He grins. "With extra fortune cookies."

"You know, you can just buy fortune cookies."

"Where's the fun in that?"

"WE'LL SEE HIM IN A WEEK," I reassure the kids as we watch Sam load his bags into his truck. "That's not very long at all, right?"

"Forever," Kevin mutters but lets Sam hug him.

"You have to put out fires far away," Kelsey says as he kisses her cheek, then blows a raspberry to make her giggle.

"That's right. But I won't be gone for that long, and then I'll be back, just like Auntie Tash said. Be good for her, hear me?"

They both nod solemnly.

"Can we watch Scooby?" Kevin asks.

"Sure. Go ahead." They run inside, and I turn to Sam. "Drive safely."

"Nah, I'm gonna be reckless and take chances."

"Smartass." I wrap my arms around his waist. "Call me later."

"Of course." His lips touch mine, and then he sinks into me, kissing me like crazy for the whole neighborhood to see. "Be good."

"*You* be good." I pat his butt as he pulls away. "I'll talk to you later."

"Okay." He pauses and kisses me once more.

"You're going to be late."

"You're trying awfully hard to get rid of me."

"Yeah, Pierre is waiting for me in the bedroom. I just have to get rid of those pesky kids."

Go. I don't want you to see me fall apart.

"Now who's the smartass?"

"Could be the truth." I grin when his eyes narrow. "I have some stuff to do when you go. And I don't want you to be late. Plus, I want you to drive safely."

I don't want to make a fool of myself and beg you to stay.

"I'm going. Have a good day."

He plants those lips on my forehead once more and then gets in the truck, waves, and pulls away.

He's gone.

I turn and walk inside, sit on the couch, and stare at the TV, but I don't really see or hear what's playing.

The rushing sound in my ears is too loud.

He's *gone.*

Yes, he's coming back. And, yes, I'm the one who told him to go.

But I'll miss him.

"Why are you crying?" Kelsey asks as she slips into my lap, framing my face with her tiny hands. "Are you sad?"

"A little." I wipe a tear off my cheek and smile at her. "But I'm okay."

"Do you want to snuggle my Teddy?"

"Nah, I think I'll just snuggle you." I tug her close and breathe in her sweet smell. She's so little. So sweet.

And it's just the three of us against the world now.

"Maybe you need a cookie," Kevin says.

"Do *you* want a cookie?" I ask him.

"If it makes you feel better for me to eat a cookie with you, that would be okay."

I laugh and set Kelsey on her feet, taking their hands. "We have one snafu. No cookies in the house. I guess we'll have to make some, huh?"

"With chocolate chips!" Kelsey exclaims.

"We can do that. Just no sprinkles or anything shaped like Santa. I've had my fill of that for a whole year."

"Chocolate chips are circles," Kevin says like I've lost my mind. "Not Santa."

"True that. Okay, let's get started."

"Maybe, if it'll make you feel better, we can have hot chocolate, too." Kevin's grin is sly and wide.

"You're a con artist." I kiss his head. "But you have good ideas."

CHAPTER 18

~SAM~

*T*he roads suck. I should have realized that I'd run into snow and ice on the highway in early January. It slows me up a bit.

It'll probably add an extra hour to the drive. Tash was right, I should have left earlier. I'm supposed to meet with the chief at the station at three this afternoon.

Being late on day one isn't the best way to make a first impression.

And I'm *never* late.

But leaving Tash and the kids was torture.

"I'm fucking up." I rub my hand over my mouth. "I should be there."

I tap the screen on my truck and listen as the phone rings on the other end.

"Hello?" Tash says. I can hear the smile in her voice.

"Hey, babe. What are you doing?"

"The kids and I made cookies and then we had some hot chocolate because I'm a horrible parent who gives the kids loads of sugar. Now, we're building stuff with the blocks Kevin got for Christmas. Are you there already? You made good time."

"No, I'm about halfway there. The roads are shit, so I'm taking it slow."

"Oh, no. Be careful. You shouldn't be talking to me."

"I need to." I blow out a breath. I should have had this talk with her weeks ago. "Maybe I should turn around and come home."

"Why? Did you forget something?"

Yes, damn it, I left you *behind.*

"I just think that I should be there. Maybe I made a mistake in taking the job, Tash."

"Sam, we're fine. Honest." She says something to the kids, and then I hear her walking away from them. "Don't worry about us."

Of course, I'm going to worry about them.

"Maybe I've changed my mind. Maybe it's not my dream job."

"Right. And pigs fly. Sam Waters, you've been talking about this for *years.* Now, I want you to take a deep breath and remember how hard you've worked over the past few years. You've worked your *ass* off. You put it all on hold for too long. This is a great opportunity for you."

How does she always know the right thing to say?

"Send me cookies," I reply softly. She makes the best fucking cookies I've ever had.

I can only admit that because my mom is dead and it won't hurt her feelings.

"I'll send you all the cookies you want. I should have made some for the road. I guess we'll just figure this out more and more as time goes on, right?"

I smile at the optimism in her voice.

"Yeah. I guess so. I'll send you the mailing address when I get there."

"Are you still bunking with the guy you know?"

"That's the plan. He's single, and if I'm only in town a week at a time, most of that at the station, I don't really see a need to get a place."

"Well, just get there safely, get settled, and then call me. Sam, it's going to be awesome, and we'll be fine. Just think of all the phone sex we can have."

"That's a bonus." I laugh, feeling better. "Thanks for the pep talk, babe."

"Anytime. The kids are arguing again, so I have to go be the referee. I love you."

"I love y—" Before I can finish the sentence, she hangs up.

I already miss her. But she's right, we'll figure it out. And I'm excited for everything I'm going to learn at this new job.

It's just nerves.

∾

"Sam's the new guy, so he's buying," Charlie says with a laugh as we walk into the bar after our shift. The six of us sit at a booth, order massive quantities of wings and beer, and settle in to watch a game and razz each other.

After just two days on the job, this is the new routine.

I'm hardly at my buddy's place. I'm either at the station, or out with these guys. They're harmless, and letting off steam is good for us.

Some of the shit I've already seen since I've been here isn't for the faint of heart.

"I've been the new guy the last two nights, as well," I remind Charlie, who just grins.

"Doesn't make you any less of the new guy."

"I'm not buying you shit," I respond but clink my beer bottle to his. "You can buy mine. I pulled your ass out of that building this morning."

His face sobers. "Deal."

My phone buzzes in my pocket. I pull it out and see Natasha's name on the screen. Guilt moves through me.

Aside from a brief conversation the night I arrived, I've barely talked to her. It's been mostly text messages, and even those are few and far between.

It's not at all what I envisioned when I left her house the other morning.

But I'm busier than I expected. Between calls and training, there just hasn't been a break.

I send her to voicemail. I wouldn't be able to hear her if I took the call in here, but I'll be sure to call her back when we leave.

"Everything okay?" Charlie asks.

"Aside from long-distance relationships sucking ass? Yeah, everything's fine."

"If this is the life you want, relationships are hard, period," Diego says. He has to be fifty, but he's incredibly fit with a handlebar mustache streaked with silver. "We have crazy hours, and it's just fucking demanding."

"I'm used to crazy hours," I remind him. "And I think some guys can have good relationships."

"Our job *is* a mistress," Diego responds. "And it's one that most women don't want to compete with. I live and breathe this job."

I nod. I know other men in Cunningham Falls with similar philosophies.

But I believe, if you work at it, you can balance both.

The conversation shifts to the football championship happening next month. It falls on my week off, and I'm looking forward to being home for it.

Hell, I'm just looking forward to being *home.*

I glance down when my phone lights up again and frown.

"Something's wrong." I slide out of the booth. "I'll be right back."

I hurry out the front door to the sidewalk and answer.

"Hey."

"Hi. I hope you're not too busy."

"I was having dinner. What's up?"

There's a pause.

"I'm sorry to interrupt your dinner. It's nothing I can't handle. I'll talk to you later."

"Whoa, wait."

But she's already hung up.

I take a deep breath and dial her number.

"I told you, I have it."

"What, exactly, is *it*?"

"My car died again. I had to walk a mile and a half, and it's damn cold outside, but I've been carrying more layers in the car, just in case."

"I thought it was fixed."

"So did I. Obviously, not."

"You need a new car."

"Right." She scoffs. "I'll get right on that. Listen, I just wanted to fill you in. Go eat. What are you having?"

"Wings and beer with the guys."

Another pause. "Oh. Well, go enjoy your night out, then. Talk to you later."

She hangs up, and I want to kick something.

Why should I feel guilty for going out for dinner after a shift? And why should she be mad about it? It's ridiculous.

But rather than have a long conversation about it, I pocket my phone and walk back into the restaurant to finish dinner.

I'll talk with Natasha later.

I HAVE ROUGHLY twelve hours to go before I can get in the truck and head home. I miss the kids like crazy. It seems whenever I FaceTime in the evening, they're already in bed.

And don't even get me started on how much I miss Tash. I want to touch her. Kiss her. Shit, I just want to be with her.

I'm sure that what I have is an old-fashioned case of homesickness, but it sucks ass, and I'm ready to get back home.

One more shift.

I can do it.

I've just started going down my list of things to do when I first arrive when the chief pokes his head out of his office. "Waters, I need you for a minute."

"Sure, Chief."

I walk inside, and he shuts the door.

"Am I fired already?"

"No." He laughs and shakes his head. "No, things are going well. I just needed to let you know that I need you next week. Diego is taking the week off, and I have some more training for you."

"So, no week off."

"No can do," he says absently. "But the upside is that the overtime pay doesn't suck, right?"

"Sure." I wipe my hand over my face.

"You'll have tomorrow off, and then I need you back here the following morning, same time as usual."

"Got it." I nod and stand, then leave his office and dread the call I'm about to make.

I dial her number and wait for just a second before Natasha answers.

"Hey there," she says, her voice light for the first time since I left last week. "I'm so glad you called because I'm about to go to the grocery, and I'm going to buy steaks for dinner tomorrow night. Do you want a ribeye or a sirloin?"

"Listen, babe, about that—"

"If you're not in the mood for steak, I can make something else. Would you rather have lasagna? Kelsey was asking for that the other day."

"It's not that. Tash, take a breath and let me get a word in, okay?"

"Sorry." She giggles. "I'm just excited."

My heart hurts. "I know. I was too. Look, the chief just pulled me into his office."

I fill her in on the new development.

"Oh."

I hear the defeat in her voice and feel like shit.

"I'm sorry. I had no idea."

"I know. It's not your fault." Her voice is hollow. "We'll just see you next week."

"Well, that's my usual week on, so it'll likely be another two weeks."

There's a pause. "Right. Of course."

"Sweetheart, I'm so sorry."

"Don't be silly." I hear the tears in her voice. "It's your job, Sam. These things happen, especially when you're the new guy. It makes sense they'd want you to fill in for vacations and stuff after you had to wait so long to go out there. They probably had to wait for their time off."

"Yeah, that's what I figure, too, but I should have thought of it. I'm an asshole for not realizing."

"It's okay." She clears her throat. "We've already made it one week. We just have to do this twice more and you'll be here. No big deal."

It's a big deal. I can hear in her voice that she's full of shit.

It's a big fucking deal.

"Tash—"

"Oh, I've got another call coming in I have to take. Thanks for letting me know, Sam. Love you."

She clicks off.

Fuck.

CHAPTER 19

~NATASHA~

"*G*ive me the spoon." I hold my hand out toward Kevin, but he stares me in the eye with a frown on his adorable little face and then runs away with the utensil. "We have to go to school! Come back here."

He's done with his cereal. Why is he running around this house with the spoon? Just to drive me crazy?

Make me cry?

Because I've cried more in the past month than I have since Monica died, and that's saying quite a lot.

"Kevin, if you don't want me to be homicidal, you'll put that spoon in the sink and get your damn shoes on so we can walk to school."

"You're not supposed to swear," he yells back.

I take a deep breath.

I don't feel well. I've been chilled and nauseated all

morning. I want to crawl into bed and stay under the covers.

But I can't. I have to walk the kids to school because my car is on the fritz, and the law says they have to attend school.

"Let's go," I call back. "*Now.*"

They know this voice. It's that of a woman on the edge. And they don't usually argue when I've had to pull it out of my pocket and use it. After what feels like a damn hour, the kids are finally bundled up and ready to go.

The walk to school really isn't that bad. It's about four blocks, and the weather is mild today—no wind or snow.

If I didn't feel like hell, I'd say it's a nice day.

"I think school is stupid," Kevin grumbles.

"Extra-stupid," Kelsey agrees.

They've slipped back into being difficult and angry like they were over the summer.

We haven't seen Sam in a month, and they're acting out. They miss him.

Hell, *I* miss him.

But none of us can control his schedule.

Of course, two five-year-olds who already have insecurities from losing their parents don't understand.

"Okay, be good, do you hear me? I don't feel well today, you guys. Please just get through the day without anything crazy happening."

"Bye," Kevin says and runs off, not acknowledging me.

Kelsey waves and follows her brother.

"That went well." I walk over to a bench and sit down, too tired to tackle the four blocks back home. Maybe I'll just slip away from hypothermia out here. It's not a bad way to go.

You just fall asleep.

Not that I want to die. I just feel like crap.

"Tash."

I glance up and see Fallon standing on the sidewalk.

"Honey, you don't look so good."

"I don't *feel* so good."

"Where's your car?"

"At home." I point in the general direction of my house. "Doesn't run well right now."

"Come on, let me take you home."

I don't argue. I'm not stupid enough to try to pretend that I'm okay.

There's absolutely nothing about me that feels okay right now.

"What's going on?"

"I don't know." I rub my forehead. "I must just have a bug of some kind. I won't breathe on you."

"I'll pick the kids up from school and take them home with me."

"No." I reach out and pat her arm. "I love you for offering, but you don't have to do that. However, if you'd pick them up and bring them home, I'd appreciate it."

"I can do that. Just let me know if you change your mind about the rest. Honest, I don't mind."

She pulls into my driveway, and I muster up the energy to thank her and walk into the house, straight back to my bed. I don't bother to get undressed, I just climb between the sheets and huddle down.

I'm so *cold.*

And I just don't feel well.

I want Monica.

I feel like I'm failing with the kids, and I'm lonely. I want to have a fucking conversation with my best friend.

I want to tell her that her brother is a big jerk. Even though he's *not* a jerk. She would get what I mean.

And I want to ask questions about the kids. *Why* do certain things make Kevin so angry? Kelsey tells me I don't tuck her in right, but I don't know what the *right* way is.

I need to ask Monica.

And I can't.

I'm blubbering under the covers when I hear someone walking down the hallway.

"I have a gun," I call out weakly.

"Yeah, you scare me." Gage appears in the doorway. "You look like shit."

"I feel like shit. What are you doing here?"

"Fallon called. It's a good thing she did. You need me."

My bottom lip wobbles as I reach for my brother, but before he can sit next to me, I have to throw back the covers and run for the bathroom.

Oh, God. I'm dying.

"Whoa there," Gage says. I can hear the water running, and suddenly, there's a cool cloth on the back of my neck.

"You should go," I say and reach for toilet paper to wipe my mouth. "I'm probably contagious."

"Not leaving. You can't take care of yourself, much less those kids. You're stuck with me."

He helps me get all cleaned up and then back to bed.

"I can't do this," I mutter as I sit up in bed. "I don't know why I thought I could do this."

"Do what, exactly?" My brother moves the bench from the end of the bed and sits next to me.

"So, Sam's been gone for a month. A long, shitty month. And it's been really...lonely. Especially because I don't work, so I don't get to see other people during the day." I take the water Gage offers and take a swig. "Well, Sam got me a day at the salon for Christmas, and I went a couple of weeks ago. It was *so nice.* And not nearly as hard to be in the salon without Monica as I thought it would be. I mean, it was weird at first, but the longer I was in there, the more I kind of got over it. You know?"

"Sure."

"Well, I was talking to Reagan, the new owner, and she told me that she could use a nail tech two days a week. I mean, that's not bad. And I can make my own hours on those two days so I can just go right after dropping the kids off at school and make sure I'm finished when they get out."

"Sounds reasonable to me."

My eyes fill. "I thought so. But, I can't. The kids have been *so bad*, Gage. I've had to go to the school several times a week since they went back after winter break. They're acting out, and they're just so angry since Sam left. It's like it was last summer after their parents died."

"It doesn't help that Sam hasn't been able to come home like he promised he would."

I want to jump in and defend Sam, but I pause. "I tried to call him last night because I didn't feel good, and I just wanted to hear his voice, you know?"

Gage nods as I wipe my nose.

"He answered, but I could hear noise in the background, and he was laughing with his buddies. So, I told him I'd talk to him another time."

"If you don't want him going out with his friends, just tell him so."

"It's not that." I scoot down in bed, feeling woozy again. "I don't care if he has dinner and drinks with the guys. I trust him. He's just having a meal and letting off some steam."

"Then what's the problem?"

I sigh. "I just don't hear from him much. The kids hardly *ever* get to talk to him because they're in bed when he does call. Being a single parent is hard, Gage. So much harder than I thought it would be. And he's not here. Which brings me back around to the job. With the school calling all the time, and the other things that can go wrong, how can I commit to a job?"

"Single parents work every day, Tash."

"How? How do they manage it? Without Sam here to help pick up some slack, I don't see how I can do it."

"You have people here to help you," he reminds me. "A community of them. Hell, Fallon and Noah would help in a heartbeat, and you always have me."

"You have a life," I say softly. "I'm sure you'll be working soon, as well."

"Actually, I do have something lined up."

"What is it? And why didn't you tell me?"

"I just firmed up plans yesterday. Do you know Tate Donovan?"

I feel my eyes widen. "Of course, I do."

"Well, she's determined to walk," he says. "She wants to hire a full-time trainer to help her."

"You're *perfect* for that," I reply with as much enthusiasm as I can muster. "With all of your medical training in the Army, you'll be awesome."

"She has a long road ahead, but I think we can get her there. The point is, I might have a job, but I can always help you. You need to take that job, if it's what you want."

"I do want it." I swallow and close my eyes. "Honestly, I *need* it. Sam started paying the rent about a month ago, but I went through a lot of my savings before then."

"Why wasn't he paying before?"

"I wouldn't let him." I shrug. "It's my place, my name on the lease. And I didn't know if he'd stay."

"You're so damn stubborn," Gage says. "Take the job. It'll be good for your mental health."

Before I can answer, my phone rings.

I groan.

"It's the school. Hello?"

"Hi, Natasha, this is Callie, the school nurse. Both kids are in here, not feeling well. Kevin threw up, and Kelsey is awfully pale."

My eyes find Gage's. "I think it's going through my house. Callie, I need to have my brother pick them up. I'm sick in bed as we speak."

"Do we have him on the official paperwork as an authorized adult?"

I frown. "I'm verbally telling you that I give him permission to bring them home."

"I'm sorry. Unless he's on the paperwork, you'll have to come to get them."

Gage swears, and I sigh.

"Fine. I'll be there soon."

I hang up and stare at my brother.

"See? This is why I shouldn't take the job."

"Bullshit. Put me on the paperwork. Add Fallon and Noah. Hell, add Aspen, too. This won't happen again."

THANK GOD FOR MY BROTHER.

It's been two days, and I think we're out of the woods, but they were scary.

Kevin, Kelsey, and I piled in my bed for the sickfest, and Gage helped me keep us all clean and hydrated.

I don't think I could have done it without him.

Sam is supposed to come home today, but I'm not getting my hopes up. The last time he was supposed to come home, he was just getting off shift and the chief told him he had to stay for something or other.

So, until he pulls into the driveway, I'm not getting my hopes up at all.

"Why do we have to go to school?" Kevin asks. "Uncle Sam is coming home today, and I want to see him."

"You'll get to see him after school," I reply. "And all evening. He's going to be here for *ten* days, so there will be lots of time with him, I promise."

Suddenly, the front door opens, and Sam walks in, surprising all of us.

"Uncle Sam!" the kids exclaim and run to him, flinging themselves into his arms. "You're here!"

"Thank goodness I'm here." He kisses their faces and smiles at me. "Hey, baby."

"Hi." I need to talk to him. I've been doing a lot of thinking, and he and I need to sit down and have a heart-to-heart.

Today.

"We don't have to go to school, right?" Kevin asks hopefully.

"Unfortunately, you do. You were out too long from being sick, and you can't miss any more time."

"Wait, he was sick?" Sam scowls at me. "Why didn't you tell me?"

"I'd rather not deck you just after you arrived home." I narrow my eyes at him. "Come on, guys, let's walk to school."

"Why are you walking? It's snowing out there."

"My car isn't running," I remind him. "It's not far."

"I'll take them." He shakes his head and pulls his keys out of his pocket. "Come on, guys."

"When you get back, we need to talk," I inform him.

"Sure, sounds good. I just have to run up on the mountain really fast to help Liam with something, and then I'll be back. Okay?"

No. No, it's not okay.

It's *not* fucking fine.

But I just smile thinly. "Sure."

"Okay, see you in a bit." He kisses my cheek and then herds the kids out to the truck.

He didn't even *kiss* me properly when he saw me.

He's a fucking stranger.

This is not what I signed on for.

CHAPTER 20

~SAM~

"Sorry it took longer than I thought," Liam says with a cringe. "I know you just got back. This could have waited."

"Don't worry about it." I shake my head as we walk out to my truck. "Are we on for the big game this weekend?"

"Hell, yes," he says with a grin. "Why do you think Ellie and I came back to town? They don't exactly celebrate this sacred holiday in England the way we do here."

"Imagine that." I laugh and clap him on the shoulder. "It's good to see you. It's good to be *home.*"

"How are things in Spokane?"

"It's been interesting." I rub my hand over the back of my neck. "It sucked at first. I was damn homesick for Tash and the kids, but I found a rhythm there. A routine. The job is great, and I'm learning a lot. So, I think I'm finally over the hardest part. And Tash has been a superstar. She just has everything under control and assures me that everything's fine."

"That's awesome," Liam replies. "I'm damn happy for you."

"Thanks. I'd better get back to the house and spend some time with her."

"I'll see you on Sunday." He taps the hood of the truck and turns back to the house as I pull out of the driveway and make my way down the mountain and back to town.

I'm so fucking proud of Natasha. I know it can't be easy taking care of everything on her own, but she never complains. I'm going to strip her naked and thank her in a thousand, sexy-as-hell ways.

I pull into the driveway and get out of the truck, then walk through the front door and pause at the sight of several bags sitting in the middle of the living room.

"Are you going somewhere?" I ask Tash with a raised brow.

"No." She clears her throat. Her eyes are flat as she stares at me. "You are. That's all of your stuff. I'm sure there are at least a half-dozen different places you can stay if you don't want to just head back to Spokane."

"Hold up." I raise a hand and narrow my eyes at her. "Talk to me."

"I can't do this," she says softly and rubs her hands

over her face. "None of what's happened in the past month is what I signed on for."

My stomach knots up and my heart starts to race. "I remember someone telling me that we'd be fine as long as we were together."

"We're not together." She stares at me as if I've grown a second head. "If you consider everything that's gone down in the past month as *together*, you're delusional."

"What are you talking about?"

"My car is *dead*, so I can't drive anywhere. I walk the kids to school. I have groceries delivered."

"I told you to get a different car."

"Right." She nods and starts pacing the living room. "Because it's just that easy, right? That's not even the worst part. The kids are doing *horribly*. They're angry and moody and *sad*. They're acting out at school again, and I get called at *least* three times a week. They miss you and ask for you. And you always manage to call when they've *just* gone to bed. What the hell is that about?

"We were so sick just a few days ago. I could hardly get my ass out of bed. I had to walk them to school that first morning, and then I just sat on a bench and hoped that hypothermia took me, so I didn't have to walk home. Luckily, Fallon saw me and brought me home. I haven't been that sick in *years*. And then, just a couple of hours later, the kids got it too, and I got called. Gage was here, thankfully, helping me out, and I told them he would pick them up.

"That was a huge *no-go*. So, I had to get my sick ass out of bed and go collect the kids. We just lived in my bed for a few days, miserable together. Thank God for my brother, Sam. I couldn't have done it by myself."

I'm just listening and shaking my head as her words hit me like little bullets.

"Why is this the first that I'm hearing of this?"

She whirls on me, her eyes shooting daggers. "Because you don't answer my fucking calls!"

Her chest is heaving, her eyes full of tears.

Thank God they're not flat anymore.

"Tash—"

"No. I don't want your excuses. I call, I text, and I tell you that I need to talk to you, but you don't respond."

"I did respond," I reply, keeping my voice calm. "I asked if it was urgent. You always say no."

"That doesn't mean you *never* call me back, you big jerk." She scrubs her hands through her hair. "It means finish what you're doing and then *call me*. But what it boils down to is really simple, Sam. You don't *want* to call. If you did, I'd hear from you more than a few times a week when you're falling asleep. You didn't even *kiss* me when you walked in. I don't feel close to you at all. And if I'm going to be a single parent and muddle my way through angry kids and broken cars without you here, I'll do it as a single woman. Because I've been miserable this month."

"You never said anything."

"I did. You didn't listen. You were too wrapped up in what was going on there to take a minute and *ask* me if everything was okay. Out of sight, out of mind, right?"

Her laugh is humorless as she reaches for her purse and keys.

"Where are you going? We need to talk about this."

"Sure. Yeah, that works. But I have to go help Fallon with some things first, is that okay?" She tosses my words from this morning back at me, rolls her eyes, and slams out of the house.

Fuck.

Jesus, have I been that selfish?

I stare at the bags in the middle of the room. I'm not fucking leaving. I'm *not* moving out. If she thinks she can just break up with me like this and that I'll leave without a fight, she's the delusional one.

And just where does she get off coming at me like that? She's the one who insisted that I go to the damn job in the first place. Now she's going to change her mind, and all of this is *my* fault?

Screw that.

We're going to sit down and have this out, and I'm not waiting for her to come home. I'll go find her. She couldn't have gotten far. She's on foot, for Christ's sake.

But when I open the door, Gage is standing on the other side, his fist raised to knock.

His eyebrows climb in surprise. "You're here."

"Hello to you, too. Natasha isn't here."

"Good." He pushes his way into the house and stares at the bags. "Wow, I didn't think she'd actually kick you out."

"I don't understand what the fuck is going on here."

"Yeah, communication hasn't been your strong suit."

I glare at him and cross my arms over my chest. "I don't particularly like that she's been telling you all of the details of our life but hasn't talked to *me.*"

"Maybe you should answer a damn call once in a while." He rocks back on his heels and tucks his hands into his pockets. His eyes are angry, but his voice is calm. "She's had a shitty time of it since you left. If you called to actually *talk* to her, you'd have known that."

"We did talk." I shove my hand through my hair. "I asked how the kids were, how everything else was going. She said it was fine."

"Fine." He laughs and shakes his head at me like I'm the dumbest asshole on the Earth. "Don't you know when a woman says it's *fine* that it's not really fine? Did you ask for details?"

I think back on it and sigh. "No, because by the time I could call, I was in bed and exhausted."

"Look, I get it," Gage says. "I was in the Army, and we were busy as hell. I couldn't always call out and didn't want to. I was exhausted. I imagine it's the same for you and what you do for a living."

I nod, but he keeps going.

"The difference here is, I didn't have a woman and kids waiting around to hear from me. I didn't have to worry about a family. So, it wasn't a big deal that I didn't check in with anyone. I could be selfish."

"I'm not a selfish man."

"If you were, Tash wouldn't love you," he says. "Doesn't mean that your actions weren't selfish. It's easy to let her deal with everything when you're gone and busy with another life. Not so easy when it's shoved in your face how badly you screwed up by avoiding what was going on at home."

"I didn't consciously do that." I blow out a breath. "Maybe it is easy to let her deal with it. I honestly thought she was handling it."

"She's a strong woman," Gage agrees. "But everyone has a breaking point. I think being sick and alone a few days ago was it for her. She needed you, and you weren't here."

"You should have called me."

He stares at me coldly. "No. I shouldn't have." He steps around me to the front door. "Oh, by the way, you can't stay with me."

He leaves, and I stare at the closed door and then laugh.

I'm staying right *here*—in my own damn home.

I walk back to the bedroom and take a deep breath.

It smells like her. There's still a framed photo of us next to the bed.

She hasn't given up on us entirely.

She's frustrated, and I see now that she should be.

If I couldn't get her to answer the phone, I'd be frustrated, too.

I was afraid of this. Of all of it. It's one of the reasons I didn't think I should take the job in the first place. I should have listened to my gut and stayed put.

For all our sakes.

I pull out my phone and make the first call, which goes pretty much the way I thought it would.

I'm damn grateful.

And then I make the second call.

"Fire hall," the chief says when he answers.

"It's Waters." I sit on the end of the bed. "I know this is going to put you in a bind, and I apologize, but I'm not coming back, sir."

There's a brief pause. "What happened?"

"My life fell apart while I was gone. And, frankly, as much as I love the job, I love her more."

"Diego always tells everyone that they can't have a family *and* the job," Chief says with a sigh. "I say that's bullshit. It's hard, but you can find the balance. I'm disappointed to lose you because you're fucking good at your job. But, if I were in your shoes, I'd do the same. My life doesn't work without Lorraine."

"Thank you for understanding."

"I assume CFFD took you back?"

"I just got off the phone with them," I confirm.

"Good. I'll make some calls of my own. Good luck to you, Waters."

"Thank you, sir."

I hang up and get to work unpacking my bags, putting everything away. And then I make a call to the garage that fixed Tash's car last time.

After I make it clear that I'm not happy with the work and that I'll be letting others in town know, I'm assured that a tow truck will come to fetch the SUV and get it back in working order.

I have my mother's famous spaghetti sauce simmering on the stove before I head back to take a shower.

I'm going to win her back.

There is no other choice.

CHAPTER 21

~NATASHA~

"*J* hope he's gone when I get back. I don't want to see him again." I wipe at a tear in frustration and then take a bite of my third cookie.

Fallon and I met at Drips & Sips. Aspen isn't here because she's in London, but it's still my favorite place to come.

"Do you think he'll really move out?" Fallon asks.

"He better. I told him to." I scowl. "*My* name is on the lease."

"Are you sure you *want* to break it off?" She reaches over and takes my hand. "You've loved him *forever*."

"I still do," I admit and take another bite of cookie. "More than anything. But I don't want to be with him and do the long-distance thing. He's *not* good at it."

"Long distance is so hard," Fallon agrees. "I think you're either good at it or you're not."

"And he's *not*. I just feel bad for the kids. They lost

so much last year, and now Sam, too. I mean, of course, they'll still see him, but it's not the same. They were used to having him here, used to living as a family."

"You all were."

"Yeah. I was so stupid. I thought we'd figure it all out, but I guess I was living in fantasy land."

"I think you should talk it out with him more."

"I don't see what there is to discuss. I'm not going through even one more day like the past month, and he pretty much lives in Spokane now."

She shakes her head. "Has anyone ever told you that you're stubborn?"

I laugh and reach for cookie number four. "A few times. I guess I should stop eating cookies and head out. Get ready for the kids to come home in a few hours and the fun conversation *that's* going to be."

"I'll drive you home."

"Since it's pretty much a blizzard out there right now, I'll take you up on that."

"What are you going to do about your car?" Fallon asks as we walk out to her vehicle.

"I don't know. Probably scrap it and buy a new one. It was used when I bought it, and I knew it wouldn't last me more than a few years, but the timing is bad."

"It always is." She drives the few blocks through town to my house, and I scowl when I see that Sam's truck is still in the driveway.

Based on the amount of snow covering it, I'd say he never left.

"I don't want it to get ugly." I lay my head back on the seat. "He just needs to *go.*"

"I want you to promise me something," Fallon says before I can get out of the car. "I want you to *listen* to him. If you're still convinced that this is the right thing to do when he's done talking, fine. But at least let him say his piece."

"Fine." I sigh and stare at my front door in dread. "Thanks for the ride and for listening to me vent."

"That's what I'm here for." She grins. "Good luck."

"I think I'll need it."

I slowly walk up to the front porch and take a deep breath before opening the door.

I smell something delicious. And when I walk in, the bags I spent several hours packing this morning are gone from the living room.

"Hey," Sam says as he walks out of the kitchen. He's smiling and wraps his arms around me, then presses his lips to mine. The kiss is chaste at first but then gets more passionate until he has to back away so we can catch our breath. "Christ, I missed that."

"Uh, Sam, where are your bags?"

"Oh, I unpacked them. Everything's put away, and I got dinner started for later."

He smiles proudly.

"Did I walk into an alternate dimension?" I look around. "Sam, I broke up with you."

"Good thing it didn't stick." He winks.

"That's the whole point of breaking up. It sticks. I

told you, I don't want to do the long-distance thing with you anymore, and—"

"Good. Me, either."

I stop and stare at him. "Huh?"

"I already called Spokane. I'm not going back."

"No." I shake my head and pace away.

"Already been hired back on here, too."

"Sam, I'm not going to be the reason you give up on your dream."

"Tash, don't you get it? *You* are my dream. You and the kids are everything I want. If you're miserable, then I am, too. And I should have done a much better job of making sure that you three were well taken care of while I was gone. That's on me, and it's something I'll have to live with."

He brushes a piece of my hair off my cheek and cups my jawline.

"I'm sorry that I fucked it all up so badly. But I'll be damned if I'll give up and leave. Not for a job, not for *anything.* I love you so much, I can't breathe from the heaviness of it. And I need you. I need the kids."

"I need you, too," I whisper, and for the first time in weeks, I feel *hope* settle in my chest. "I know I was the one who pushed you to take the job, and then I bailed. But it was just so awful, Sam."

"I'm fixing that right now. Your car's already back in the shop, and if they fuck it up again, it's going in the trash heap, and I'm buying you a new one. We'll sit down with the kids tonight to discuss their attitudes. You're not alone in this, baby. You never have been."

I jump against him and wrap my arms around his neck.

"I'm so relieved." He hugs me back. "Oh, and I have a new job."

He pulls back and stares down at me. "Lots of changes lately."

"Not all bad." I tip my forehead against his. "Thank you. Thank you for doing all of this."

"Thank you for not stabbing me this morning." He kisses my nose. "How long do we have before the kids get out of school?"

I check my watch. "About two hours."

"We'd better get started, then." He lifts me and hurries to the bedroom. "I have a lot of time to make up for."

"I mean, we never even had phone sex."

"What I have in mind is much, much better." He lays me on the bed but doesn't undress me. He just kisses me long and slow. "Now, let's spend some time in the slow lane."

"As long as we make it to the fast lane, too."

EPILOGUE

~NATASHA~

Six Months Later...

"$\mathcal{W}$ho's excited for burgers?" I ask as the four of us climb out of Sam's truck to walk into Ed's for dinner.

"Me!" Kelsey exclaims as she takes my hand. "I want extra fries."

"You're my French fry monster." I grin down at her.

The kids have grown like weeds in the last year. And since Sam came home to stay, they've thrived. Now that it's summer, we're looking forward to spending time on the lake and hiking up in the woods together as a family.

We walk inside and are shown to a booth. As we walk through the restaurant, I notice that Aspen,

Callum, and their kids are at a table. I wave, excited to see them.

I thought they were in London.

I scoot into the booth, and Sam sits next to me on the outside as I glance around. "Sam, Aspen and Callum are in town."

"Yeah? That's great."

"She didn't call me. She *always* tells me when she's coming to town."

"Maybe it was a last-minute trip," he says with a shrug.

I look to our right and see Nina and Sebastian, and not far from them are Liam and Ellie.

My brother is at the counter with Seth King next to him.

Noah and Fallon are behind us.

The rest of the King family, the *entire* King family is seated throughout the restaurant. It's a packed house, full of all of the faces I love the most.

"Why are all of our friends here?" I ask.

They're all grinning but trying not to look at us.

"Because Sam told them to," Kevin says, earning a glare from Sam. "I mean, I don't know."

I look at the man I love and notice that he looks…*nervous.*

He clears his throat and then looks over at me with the most intense blue eyes I've ever seen.

He slips his hand into his pocket and seamlessly shifts onto one knee at the side of the booth, then reaches for my hand and slides me on the bench seat next to him.

"I love you, Natasha Mills. For a million and one reasons, all of which I will list for you later." He winks. "I don't know that I could have made it through the past year with all of its intense ups and downs with anyone but you. You brought so much light and balance to my life, so much strength and love. I don't ever want to know a day without you in it."

He slips the ring out of his hand and holds it up to me.

The diamond sparkles in the light.

"Will you please marry me?"

"Of course." I wrap my arms around his neck and bury my face against him. "Of course, I'll marry you."

The entire restaurant explodes with applause. Even Ed grins from ear to ear behind the counter.

"Onion rings on me," he calls out, making me laugh.

"We're getting married," Kelsey exclaims. "I told you she was gonna say yes."

Sam stands and pulls me with him so we can get caught up in the sea of our friends for congratulations and well-wishes.

And I know in my heart that Monica and Rich are with us. Celebrating, too. Proud of the family we've made.

I can't wait for the rest of my life.

NEWSLETTER SIGN UP

I hope you enjoyed reading this story as much as I enjoyed writing it! For upcoming book news, be sure to join my newsletter! I promise I will only send you news-filled mail, and none of the spam. You can sign up here:

https://mailchi.mp/kristenproby.com/ newsletter-sign-up

ALSO BY KRISTEN PROBY:

Other Books by Kristen Proby

The With Me In Seattle Series

Come Away With Me
Under The Mistletoe With Me
Fight With Me
Play With Me
Rock With Me
Safe With Me
Tied With Me
Breathe With Me
Forever With Me
Stay With Me
Indulge With Me
Love With Me
Dance With Me

Dream With Me
You Belong With Me
Imagine With Me
Shine With Me
Escape With Me

Check out the full series here: https://www.
kristenprobyauthor.com/with-me-in-seattle

The Big Sky Universe

Love Under the Big Sky
Loving Cara
Seducing Lauren
Falling for Jillian
Saving Grace

The Big Sky
Charming Hannah
Kissing Jenna
Waiting for Willa
Soaring With Fallon

Big Sky Royal
Enchanting Sebastian
Enticing Liam
Taunting Callum

Heroes of Big Sky

Honor

Courage

Check out the full Big Sky universe here: https://www.kristenprobyauthor.com/under-the-big-sky

Bayou Magic

Shadows

Spells

Check out the full series here: https://www.kristenprobyauthor.com/bayou-magic

The Romancing Manhattan Series

All the Way

All it Takes

After All

Check out the full series here: https://www.kristenprobyauthor.com/romancing-manhattan

The Boudreaux Series

Easy Love

Easy Charm

Easy Melody

Easy Kisses

Easy Magic

Easy Fortune

Easy Nights

Check out the full series here: https://www. kristenprobyauthor.com/boudreaux

The Fusion Series

Listen to Me

Close to You

Blush for Me

The Beauty of Us

Savor You

Check out the full series here: https://www. kristenprobyauthor.com/fusion

From 1001 Dark Nights

Easy With You

Easy For Keeps

No Reservations

Tempting Brooke

Wonder With Me

Shine With Me

Kristen Proby's Crossover Collection

Soaring with Fallon, A Big Sky Novel

ALSO BY KRISTEN PROBY:

Wicked Force: A Wicked Horse Vegas/Big Sky Novella
By Sawyer Bennett

All Stars Fall: A Seaside Pictures/Big Sky Novella
By Rachel Van Dyken

Hold On: A Play On/Big Sky Novella
By Samantha Young

Worth Fighting For: A Warrior Fight Club/Big Sky
Novella
By Laura Kaye

Crazy Imperfect Love: A Dirty Dicks/Big Sky Novella
By K.L. Grayson

Nothing Without You: A Forever Yours/Big Sky
Novella
By Monica Murphy

Check out the entire Crossover Collection here:
https://www.kristenprobyauthor.com/kristen-proby-
crossover-collection

ABOUT THE AUTHOR

Kristen Proby has published close to fifty titles, many of which have hit the USA Today, New York Times and Wall Street Journal Bestsellers lists. She continues to self publish, best known for her With Me In Seattle and Boudreaux series, and is also proud to work with William Morrow, a division of HarperCollins, with the Fusion and Romancing Manhattan Series.

Kristen and her husband, John, make their home in her hometown of Whitefish, Montana with their two cats and dog.

facebook.com/booksbykristenproby
instagram.com/kristenproby
bookbub.com/profile/kristen-proby
goodreads.com/kristenproby